FALLING FOR AN ALIEN ELF

Holiday with a Cu'zod Warrior, Book 2

AVA ROSS

FALLING FOR AN ALIEN ELF

Book 2, Holiday with a Cu'zod Warrior Series

Copyright © 2021 Ava Ross

All rights reserved.

No part of this book may be reproduced in any form or by any electronic or mechanical means, including information storage and retrieval systems, without written permission from the author, except for the use of brief quotations with prior approval. Names, characters, events, and incidents are a product of the author's imagination. Any resemblance to an actual person, living or dead is entirely coincidental.

Cover art by Germancreative

Editing by JA Wren & Owl Eyes Proofs & Edits

AISN: B09FVKHCBS

❀ Created with Vellum

For my mom.
Thanks for believing in me.
I miss you.

Books by AVA

MAIL-ORDER BRIDES OF CRAKAIR

Vork

Bryk

Jorg

Kral

Wulf

Lyel

Axil, Gaje

(Companion novellas)

❋

BRIDES OF DRIEGON

Malac

Drace

Rashe

Teran

Kruze, Allor, Skoar

(Companion novellas)

ALIEN EMBRACE ANTHOLOGY

Skoar

(A Brides of Driegon novella

available for a limited time)

❄

FATED MATES OF THE FERLAERN WARRIORS

Enticed by an Alien Warlord

Tamed by an Alien Warlord

Seduced by an Alien Warlord

Tempted by an Alien Warlord

Craved by an Alien Warlord

❄

XILAN WARRIOR'S MATES

Alien Commander's Mate

Alien Prince's Bride

Alien Hunter's Prize

Alien Pirate's Plunder

On Kindle Vella

❄

HOLIDAY WITH A CUZ'OD WARRIOR

Snowed in with an Alien

Falling for an Alien Elf

You can find my books on Amazon.

Falling For An Alien Elf

With Christmas around the corner, can Emily and a Cu'zod alien warrior turn fake dating into a happily ever after?

Blue-skinned, scaled aliens are settling on Earth, and Emily signed on to be a sponsor. Likir will work at her animal rescue, and she'll help him transition into Earth society. But after her jerky ex cuts off her animal rescue funding right before Christmas, Emily's scrambling to find donors. When Likir spontaneously offers to be her pretend date to secure tickets to the annual Christmas Costume Ball where she'll find donors galore, she accepts. But a few stolen kisses make this feel way too real. Can Emily keep her hands off this appealing Cu'zod warrior?

Before Prince Likir moved to Earth, he ditched his royal status, determined to succeed on Earth under his own merits and not those of his illustrious family. He doesn't expect to find his sponsor the most appealing female on the planet or to find himself pretending to be her boyfriend.

The more he gets to know her, the harder he falls. Can he convince Emily to make their pretend romance real?

Falling for an Alien Elf is Book 2 in the Holiday with a Cu'zod Warrior Series. This standalone, full-length romance has on-the-page heat, aliens who look and act alien, a guaranteed happily ever after, humor, no cheating, and no cliffhanger.

1

Emily

*E*mily was late to pick up her Cu'zod alien warrior from the spaceport. They expected her promptly at four o'clock, and it was nearly that time already.

It wasn't completely her fault she was running behind.

Alfred sliced his paw on ice during his walk, and Emily had to take care of the wound before she left the poor creature alone in his pen overnight. He was bleeding. In pain. As it was, Emily would need to set her alarm for 2:00 a.m. to check the wound and make sure the dog was okay.

For now, she carried Alfred in her arms.

"Poor little fella."

Alfred was one of the unadoptables at her rescue, a Yorkie-Chihuahua mix. She assumed he got his skinny legs from his chihuahua dad and his long, black, tan, and golden hair from his Yorkie mom.

His missing eye, places where no hair would ever grow, and severed back leg came from a cruel owner.

He huffed as she nuzzled him against her throat. When he was dropped off here by the cops who'd found him in a closet during a drug raid, he'd tried to bite her throat when she got her face too close. Time and patience had rewarded her. Now, he licked her chin and grunted.

Near the exit to her tiny clinic area, she put Alfred down by her feet. He waited patiently while she secured a puppy sling around her neck and across her chest.

Once Alfred was secured inside the pouch, she left the pen wing of her business, *Grannie's Rescue*, humming along with *Walking in a Winter Wonderland* piping in from the ceiling. The animals in her rescue were soothed by music, and Emily kept it seasonal. Actually, Christmas was her favorite holiday. If she could get away with playing Christmas music all year long, she'd do it.

She hurried across the grooming area that connected to her small house, thinking of the things she still had to do before she could leave to the spaceport. A jolt, and her feet slipped out from underneath her. She cradled Alfred as she fell. Landing hard on her left hip on the wet floor, she groaned.

"Alfie, are you okay?" she cried out.

He yipped, but it held a cheerful sound, as if he'd enjoyed the unexpected ride to the floor.

Hip aching, she stared at the *Wet Floor* sign the cleaning crew had left near the door, indicating the tile was freshly mopped. As much as she hurt, she couldn't snarl at them. They left the place sparkling, and she hadn't been paying attention when she crossed the room.

Rising with a groan, she patted Alfred's tiny head and hobbled into her attached house and then to her office, where she sat at her desk and struggled not to cry. She wasn't seriously injured, but damn, her hip kept spasming. Hopefully she hadn't broken anything when she fell.

She pushed aside the pain, something she didn't have time for, and opened the bottom drawer of her desk, where she kept treats.

Alfred squirmed in the sling, and she tucked a tiny dental chew inside the pouch with him. Like always, he dragged it down into his little hidey hole and proceeded to gnaw on it.

Emily pulled her pile of paperwork closer on her desk blotter. Through stinging eyes, she studied the figures on her spreadsheet, hoping they'd add up to more money than they had yesterday. Even with a grant from her slimy ex-boyfriend, things were tight.

Quivering with worry, she closed the document and completed the rest of the urgent paperwork. When she stood, she held back her gasp at the pain. It didn't help that her clothing was still damp and sticking to her spine.

Her plan was to change quickly, jump into her beat-up Subaru, and speed to the spaceport. A few minutes late wouldn't be noted, right?

Five years ago, three male Cu'zods landed on Earth. Talk about everyone freaking out. Some Earthlings ran to rooftops with welcome signs. Others hid in bunkers with canned goods stored for what they saw as the looming apocalypse.

Others descended on California, hoping for a peek at the aliens.

One of the three aliens met and fell in love with an Earth woman. He remained on Earth, and they married and had a child. Sadly, the Earth woman and Cu'zod warrior were killed a year or so ago in a fire. Their four-year-old child was being raised by her aunt and the new Cu'zod Ambassador to Earth.

The other two aliens were captured and taken to a laboratory for experimentation. Only the intervention of Emily's government prevented an interstellar disaster. They freed the males, who returned to Cu'zod, no doubt carrying the tale of their terrifying experience. After that horror story, the Cu'zods backed away, deciding not to return to Earth.

Earthlings continued as before, with the single alien living among them until his death. Only those living near him remembered he existed.

Then, a little over a year ago, a Cu'zod delegation came to Earth and a treaty was formed. Through the treaty, Earth received technology and planet security, the Ambassador's residence was established, and the first exchanges took place, though only a few Cu'zods opted to settle on Earth and ten or so Earthlings traveled to Cu'zod.

The initial exchanges worked out so well that a regular program was initiated. Emily had applied to be a host to an alien settler, and he was waiting at the spaceport for her to pick up.

And she was late. Half an hour late, actually.

Changed into dry clothing and with Alfred in his sling, she was crossing her living room when someone knocked on her front door.

Who could it be?

She paused in the small entry to peek through the tiny hole.

Alfred's growl should've told her who was waiting on the other side.

"Ugh." Emily leaned against the wall beside the door. Could she go out the back entrance to avoid him?

"Emily," her ex-boyfriend, Bradley, called out. "I know you're in there. Your car's in the drive. Open the door, and we'll get this over with."

Alfred's growl increased in volume. She tucked her hand inside his pouch and stroked his little head. He licked her fingers.

Closing her eyes tightly, she counted to ten. Make that

twenty. She'd need the fortitude to face him, and not only because she'd hoped she'd never see him again.

He'd brought his newest girlfriend. The designer-clothed brunette clinging to his arm was cute and about fifteen years younger than his thirty-five.

He liked them young, something Emily had learned from the three women calling to fill her in on what a slime he truly was. After that, it was over. She put his things out in her driveway, changed the locks on her doors, and told him it was over.

No one ditched Bradley Williamson Davenport the third. To say he was pissed was an understatement. He'd flung his possessions around her driveway, breaking most of them, and the nasty words he shouted before he left proved all over again why she was much better off without him.

The other women he'd cheated with were talking about forming a 'we-hate-Bradley' club. Not really, but—

"Emily," Bradley barked. "I said, open the door."

She could be sleeping. Working with the eleven dogs and twelve cats and kittens in her rescue. Or taking a shower. Hell, she could be reading a good book. Anything beat interacting with Bradley.

"If you don't open up in ten seconds, I'll call your mother," he said.

Ugh. Mom loved Bradley, despite his cheating ways. Probably because Mom and Dad's lives revolved around making money, not being parents to Emily. Nope, Grannie had been the only true parent Emily grew up with.

Mom wanted Emily to beg Bradley to take her back. If Bradley called Mom, Mom would call Emily immediately.

He's handsome, she'd say.

He's got a place on the ocean in Cape Elizabeth, she'd add.

He's got more money than Midas, she'd finish off with.

Like Emily cared about anything like that? She'd fallen for the person she thought he was, not what he could give her.

"Ten… Nine…" he called out.

"Might as well get it over with," she whispered. "Find out what he wants then make him leave."

Alfred whined, and she couldn't blame him. He'd never liked Bradley, which should've told her something.

She unlocked and opened the front door. The jingle bells she'd hooked on the knob rang out merrily, making her wish Santa or an elf stood on the doorstep, not her cheating ex.

He disengaged his girlfriend's arms from around his neck and nudged her body away from his, which meant unlocking her legs from around his waist, as well. The brunette's heels clicked on the top step as he lowered her to her feet.

Emily seemed to be the only one with the grace to blush. The brunette smiled at Bradley. He grinned, enjoying Emily's discomfort.

"Really, Bradley?" Emily said, perturbed. "This is a nice neighborhood. Kids play on the sidewalks. There's no need to give them a show."

The girlfriend giggled. Bradley faked a scowl, but Emily knew him too well. He was pleased she'd caught him groping the other woman. He thought he was showing Emily that he'd moved on, that Emily meant nothing.

Who cared?

"This won't take long," he said, breezing past her into the small house she'd inherited from her grandmother. "I don't wish to keep you, though I doubt you have plans for tonight." He smirked. "Or any night, for that matter."

"Actually, I do have plans," Emily said.

Alfred poked his head from the carrier and growled.

Bradley sneered at the tiny pup. "Still have that mutt?"

"He's a good boy," she said, her heart aching for the poor creature no one but her loved.

"He bit me."

"I bet he had a good reason."

"You know he hates me," Bradley said.

Emily sighed as his girlfriend followed him inside. She strode into the living room as if she owned the place and settled on the sofa. The woman picked up the remote and turned on the TV, switching the channels until she came to an ice hockey game.

"Go Bs," she shouted, waving her arms in the air.

Alfred huffed, and Emily wished she could huff, too.

"I have a date tonight, actually," Emily said, stretching it a bit, but oh, well.

One of Bradley's eyebrows lifted. "You, a date?"

His comment shot through her like an electrical jolt. "Yes, a date. Men enjoy going out with me." A total lie. She hadn't had the heart to even smile at a guy since her Bradley disaster.

"I'd love to meet him," he said, glancing around as if he expected her "date" to pop out of the woodwork.

"He's not here right now but will be…soon." She lifted her eyebrows. "Why are *you* here?"

"Let's take this to your office, shall we?" Bradley asked.

Emily stiffened her spine. "Whatever you have to say can be said here."

His gaze shot to his girlfriend, who continued to cheer the players skating across Emily's TV screen. "I don't want to embarrass you."

Frankly, she was embarrassed she hadn't seen through him sooner.

"Just spit it out," she said.

"Very well." His piercing gaze met hers. "I'm withdrawing your funding."

"What?" She sagged against the wall. Her hip spasmed when it hit, but she ignored the pain.

"I'm no longer funding this…little project of yours."

Indignation sparked through her. "It's not a little project."

There was a time where he'd seen its value, too. Sure, he hadn't loved the dogs or cats as much as Emily did, and he'd insisted none were allowed in the bedroom, much to Alfred's dismay, but Bradley told her once that he admired her for caring for those no one else wanted.

It appeared Emily was not the only misfit in the house. Her parents had booked a trip to Tahiti—for just them—and Emily's beloved Grannie had died nine months ago.

But without funding, she'd have to ramp up her program and find forever homes for the beloved animals in her care.

"I do wonderful work here," Emily said, praying he didn't see her lower lip trembling. She wanted to rage. She wanted to cry. "You know that."

"Take them to the local animal shelter. They'll figure out what to do with them there."

Her hands fluttered at her throat. "It's a kill shelter. You know the animals I take in are not easily placed."

"That's their problem now, isn't it?" He grunted at Alfred, whose lips peeled back in a snarl. "Like this mutt. What good is he to anyone?"

"He loves me." Something Bradley and her parents did not.

"Pets love just about anyone, but why have a defective one when you could adopt a whole one?"

That made her chest burn. "Alfred and my rescue

animals are kind souls who just need help finding forever homes. They're perfect in every way."

"Well, you'll have to fund your good deeds with someone else's dollar." He turned to his girlfriend. "Honey, it's time to go."

The brunette pouted. "The third period's almost over. Can't I watch the last five minutes?"

"We can watch it at my house."

"It's nearly Christmas," Emily said. For Alfred and the other animals in her care, she'd beg. "Please don't do this."

He flashed his gleaming white smile. "The holidays are the perfect time to seek other donors. Tell them your dog and cat sob stories, and they'll open their wallets." His nose scrunched. "Except this mutt. No one will want that thing underneath their tree no matter how big the bow."

He flicked his hand toward Alfred. Alfred, ever loyal, tried to bite Bradley's finger off.

She pivoted away before the small dog caused real harm. Not that she blamed him. Bradley might not have been mean, but he sure hadn't gone out of his way to befriend the wounded pup.

"It's not easy to find funding for projects like this," Emily said, her voice thready. "Times are tough for everyone." Including her. Without his funding, she would need to mortgage the home her grandmother had left her. There was no other money available outside of begging relatives and friends, and they'd already contributed what they could afford. Even Mom and Dad threw her a hundred bucks every now and then.

Tears smarted in her eyes, but Emily blinked fast, refusing to let them fall. She could break down once he'd left. "Please, Bradley."

"I'll tell you what. I'll be generous," he said. "You have

two weeks to find alternate funding, but then, I'm cutting you off."

"How am I supposed to write grants or find donors over the holidays? Most places close down between Christmas and New Year's." She'd applied for everything she could find, with limited success. Each dollar helped, but it took a solid amount of money to run an animal rescue.

If only she'd been able to score tickets to the Christmas Costume Ball, where all the wealthy people in Emily's community gathered on Christmas eve, then she could solicit enough donations to run her rescue for years.

It wasn't meant to be. She could park out front with a sign and hope one of the attendees took pity on her cause, but they'd kick her off the country club grounds the moment they saw her.

"I guess you'd better get on this right away, then." He chuckled. "Perhaps your new boyfriend can help you."

He knew there was no boyfriend.

Fury filled her, a good thing as it shoved aside her tears.

She would never date a man with money again. Whoever said power corrupts had it wrong. It wasn't power, it was money that turned people cold. She'd seen it over and over with her parents, and now, with Bradley.

He turned toward the living room. "It's time to leave, Bridget."

Bridget grumbled but shut off the TV. She slunk off the sofa and sauntered over to where Bradley and Emily stood in the front hall.

His hand spanned the back of her tiny waist, and she leaned in for a tongue-filled kiss.

Yuck.

As much as it hurt to grovel, Emily would do it for her

cat and dog friends. "Please, Bradley. If you can't do this for me, think of the animals."

Bridget giggled and nuzzled his neck, leaning into him while bending up one leg like women did in photos.

His sneer moved from Emily to Alfred.

"Two weeks, Emily," he said. "I'll cover you two more weeks."

Taking Bridget's hand, he left.

Bridget's heels click-click-clicked on the walkway as she scurried beside him. Bradley opened the passenger car door, and she slipped into the leather interior.

Emily didn't wait to see if Bradley looked her way. She slammed her front door closed and locked it, then slid down the back of the panel, wincing when her sore hip impacted with the hardwood floor.

She buried her face in Alfred's fur and cried.

2

Likir

"I'm terribly sorry," the Earth liaison of the exchange program, Derrick, said. He consulted his electronic device, squinting at the screen. "Your host... Ms. Carlisle, was told the time and should've been here by now."

"It isn't a problem," Likir said easily. "I'm sure she'll arrive soon."

They sat in the spaceport lounge, sipping an appalling drink called Coo-coo Coola. Why anyone would drink something like this was beyond Likir. Was this why all Earthlings had stunted growth? During his prior and this journey to Earth, he'd met no one with the lofty height of a Cu'zod.

They'd been waiting in the lounge long enough for Derrick to drink two Coo-coo Coolas. One by one, host sponsors arrived to collect their Cu'zod charges from their Earth liaisons. Nearly one hundred Cu'zods had arrived today, but only Likir remained, waiting with Derrick.

Overhead, childish voices chirped something about being on an island of misfit toys. The poor souls. Would anyone come save them from their torture chamber mounted in the ceiling? If the creatures remained trapped inside the circular box for much longer without assistance, Likir would do this himself.

"We will, of course, arrange for another host if she doesn't arrive soon," Derrick said.

"We have time."

"It's an insult, frankly. If your government discovers…" Derrick shook his head, and the hair from his tail of the pony at the base of his neck swayed on his lean back. He shifted his legs as he sat in the lounge chair opposite Likir. "It could be an intergalactic incident!"

"Our royal family will not be insulted." This, Likir knew quite well.

"You really can't tell how anyone else will act." Derrick's gaze dashed down Likir's frame, though not in an insulting way. "What did you tell me you did on Cu'zod?"

Likir hadn't said. Actually, he'd come to Earth under a secret identity. The only part of his Cu'zod persona he'd kept was his first name.

If the Earth governments discovered he was *Prince* Likir, first in line for the Cu'zod throne, they would insist on assigning security details to him, gifting him with elite living quarters, and the press would follow him around everywhere, never giving him a moment's peace.

So, instead of Prince Likir Hidaell Drukvals Yos'ae landing on this planet in the fourth Cu'zod settlement group, plain old Likir Thuzok had come instead.

This was his request, and his family had honored it so far.

"I…was a farmer," Likir finally said. More or less. The royal family did manage many farms and employ numerous farmers deep within the Brestial Sea where his people made their homes. Likir had worked alongside them from the time he was a stripling.

Above Likir and Derrick, the tiny creatures trapped in the circular box started chirping again, this time a nightmarish tale about their grandmother being stomped upon by a reign-dire. Likir would watch out for this rein-dire creature in case it attacked. Perhaps he should remove his sword from his bag for protection, though his thumb claws, tail, and horns could do considerable damage.

So far, no one had appeared to rescue the creatures singing their tales of woe. Even Derrick did not appear upset by their ongoing captivity.

"A farmer, eh?" Derrick said. "Then I guess it's good we hooked you up with someone who runs a shelter for animals." Derrick coughed. "Not exactly hooking up, that is, but you know what I mean."

Actually, no, but Likir wasn't sure it mattered.

Today, he was supposed to meet his host, the person who would help smooth his transition on Earth. This person would provide him shelter, a job, and eventually help him obtain his own living quarters. From there, he would remain on Earth, living as an Earthling.

Likir couldn't wait. Breaking free from the expectations of being royal was all he'd ever wanted. Caring for his people on Cu'zod was not the issue; formal functions and living a life in the public eye was.

"Did you own a farm on Cu'zod?" Derrick asked.

"One could say that."

"I guess you must if you worked with animals. After hearing you all live underwater, I can't imagine what kind of creatures you have on Cu'zod. Guess we'll be hearing about that when we start getting reports back from the Earthlings who've settled on your planet."

"I imagine you will."

With a polite nod, Derrick got up and strolled to one of a series of rectangular boxes standing along one wall. Colorful food items could be seen through the clear material fronting the boxes. Earlier, Derrick had inserted money and the Coo-coo Coola was projected outward, dropping to the bottom of the machine.

"Want anything?" Derrick asked, turning to glance Likir's way.

After the Coo-coo Coola, no.

"Chips? Candy bar?" Derrick added.

"I am…not hungry. Thank you," Likir said, assuming those items must be some sort of Earthling food.

"I bet your host will give you dinner later, assuming she ever gets here to pick you up."

"You are most likely correct."

What would his next few days be like? Nothing like his life on Cu'zod, that was for sure. To think all Earthlings lived above the water, on land masses. While many had left the sea on Cu'zod, his people's history was grounded beneath the waves.

His family had argued with his plan, saying he was foolish to abdicate his position in line for the throne to settle on an archaic planet. They offered him a dukedom to placate him, but what need did he have for something like that?

His older brother had mated, and they had a stripling on the way. If Likir knew his brother, this one wouldn't be their last. Each stripling they produced set Likir further from the throne, and he couldn't be happier. He wanted to be a regular male, not a prince on display.

"I'm so sorry," a female voice said from the doorway. "I got tied up with a few things but flew here as fast as I could."

Likir had not heard Earthlings drove spacecraft or had wings. Interesting.

Derrick turned, a bar of the candy—Likir presumed—in his hand. "This doesn't look good, you know, miss."

Likir stood to face her.

"I really am sorry." Pink suffused her medium-toned, attractive face. She hurried over and stood in front of Likir while Derrick did… Likir was not sure, because he couldn't stop staring at her.

She wore a sack bound to the front of her chest, and it…shifted as if something lived beneath the outer layer.

"As I said, a few things came up and… Well, I…" She held out her hand to Likir. "I'm Emily Carlisle. You're Likir, I assume?"

Ah, yes, one was supposed to latch onto a stranger's hand and pump it up and down to show greetings. Such a strange custom.

"Likir Thuzok." He took her hand, and at their touch, heat flared up his fingers. He ripped himself away, and she frowned as he essentially staggered backward.

This… He lifted his hand, staring at his fingers, but didn't see anything to explain the shock he'd received.

The pouch on her chest shifted again, and his gaze was caught again by the action.

"So happy to meet you, Likir," she said, her smile fading.

"Well, no problem. At least you got here," Derrick said. "I was going to call soon. You do know that—"

"This is not an issue," Likir said, cutting Derrick off. "She has apologized, and I accept."

"Thank you," she said. "Is there any paperwork I need to sign?"

"All taken care of," Derrick said. "You read the literature we sent?"

Her gaze shifted to the side. "I have. Mostly."

"Good, good," Derrick said, opening a bright package and taking a big bite he spoke around. "Then we're all set. As long as the rules outlined in the literature are followed, there shouldn't be any problems."

"Of course," she said. Her attention landed on Likir, who'd recovered from the odd shock and stepped forward again. "I guess we can get going and let Derrick do...whatever he has planned for the rest of the day." She peered around Likir. "Did you bring any bags?"

"I have brought a few things with me, yes," Likir said, waving to the solitary sack sitting on the floor beside the sofa.

While she rushed around him and lifted it, he took in her curvy appearance. Like all Earthlings, she wasn't very tall, the top of her head reaching only to the middle of Likir's chest.

Her hips swayed, drawing his eyes, and he unabashedly stared at her ripe ass as she bent forward. It was wrong to wonder how it would feel beneath his palms, but he couldn't help it.

Her long, reddish-gold hair swung forward, along her back, and a fringe capped her forehead, so unlike a Cu'zod, who had no hair at all, only protective ridge spikes marching from his forehead to the base of his tail.

Smooth skin coated what he could see of her body, a sharp contrast to a Cu'zod's blue scales.

He'd met Earthlings before, of course, having traveled here a year ago for the signing of the Earth-Cu'zod treaty. His friend, Trexon, was now the Ambassador from Cu'zod and had mated with an Earthling. Likir had enjoyed getting to know Aida and discovering the wonders of Earthlings in general.

Trexon was not aware Likir was among the current

settlers, and Likir planned to hold off telling Trex for a few Earthling months. He wanted to do this without formal assistance, in the same way as the other Cu'zods settling here. Once he'd found his place in this world, he would get in touch with Trex and arrange for them to get together.

During his brief stay after the signing of the treaty, Likir had attended more events than he cared to count, meeting hundreds of Earthling females. They came in a plethora of colors and sizes, but none had the same impact on him as Emily. He wasn't sure why.

"I will take my bag," he said, tugging it from her grip as she straightened. "But thank you."

"All right." She smiled brightly, but the emotion wasn't reflected in her rich hazel eyes.

A tiny, one-eyed head poked out of the sack on her chest, and Derrick reeled backward, dropping his bar. It landed with a dull thud on the floor. The little head made a sharp, yipping sound and the creature struggled beneath the outer surface of the pouch.

"That... That..." Derrick shook his head. "Not to be unkind, Ms. Carlisle, but that's one damn ugly dog."

Emily's lips twisted at his words, but her face softened as she looked down at the creature. "Oh, now you've done it," she said, though not unkindly. She loosened a tie near the tiny, one-eyed beastie's neck and lifted out the three-legged, mangy creature and placed it on the floor. Its attention zoned in on the bar Derrick had dropped and it hopped around, restrained by Emily's hands.

"What the hell is it?" Derrick said, his gray eyebrows lifting.

"This is Alfred," Emily said. She clipped a thin, green band to a matching harness encasing the creature's chest and tugged it away from the bar of food. "You can't eat that, Alfred. It has chocolate."

The creature snapped and snarled, hopping around on its three legs while straining against the thin band.

"That's the most…homely dog I've ever seen," Derrick said, coming closer. He picked up his bar and tossed it into a circular bucket with a bang.

Alfred whined and sat on his butt, gazing from Emily to Likir.

"He's not homely," Emily said in a tired voice. "He's the sweetest little guy I know." Likir had a feeling she heard disparaging comments about Alfred a lot. While it might not be the most attractive creature Likir had ever seen, there was something appealing about the tiny beastie.

He knelt down and held out his hand toward it.

"Oh, careful," Emily said. "Alfred doesn't take to strangers."

Alfred hopped closer, extending his tiny snout.

"He bite?" Derrick asked, holding his hands up near his throat.

"Just nibbles," Emily said. She stooped down, her gaze meeting Likir's. "He's really a sweetie once you get to know him."

When their eyes met, something intense swirled through Likir, though he couldn't name the feeling.

"Alfred has come a long way since he came to my rescue," she said. "At first, he wouldn't let anyone near him. He snapped and tried to bite, but he had a good reason, didn't you, little guy?" Her voice rose to a higher pitch. "With patience, he's learned to trust." She stroked the creature's back, and he huffed and sniffled like an elderly male, wiggling beneath her fingers.

Alfred's big brown eye turned Likir's way, and he hobbled closer, his snout extending again until it touched Likir's longest finger. He had three, unlike Earthlings with five. It was the same with his toes, where he had one larger, clawed toe, and two smaller, equally long toes. His claws were a holdout from days when Cu'zods needed to defend themselves against predators. Likir kept his toe claws trimmed to the base, leaving only his thumb claw long.

Alfred licked Likir's finger.

"That's...amazing," Emily said with a fleeting smile that ripped through Likir in shockwaves. "Usually, he nips. He trusts me, but no one else."

Likir shrugged. "Perhaps he senses he can trust me as well?"

"That must be it." Her warm gaze socked Likir in the chest, making him flounder while she straightened, lifting Alfred. After tucking him back inside the sack on her chest, she nodded to Likir's bag. "Are you ready to go, then?"

Likir nodded.

Her gaze flicked to Derrick, who was consuming the second brown bar he'd obtained from the tall box. "Anything else?" she asked.

"Nope," Derrick said around the bite. "We'll be in touch within a few days to see if either of you have any needs and ensure that things are going well. Please don't hesitate to get in touch if you have concerns or questions. My cell number's in your paperwork." He waved the brown bar her way, and bits of it fell to the floor.

"Perfect. I'm sure everything will go fine." When she looked Likir's way, her smile grew anew.

It hit him in the chest, stealing his breath.

To distract himself, he decided to rescue the chirping creatures in the circular device mounted on the ceiling.

As a keeper of beasts, Emily would understand. It was wrong for the tiny creatures to remain trapped inside, telling their tales of woe to whoever would listen. At the moment, they chirped about being a poor boy with no gifts to bring, pa-rum pum pum pum. Sad that they believed they must always bear gifts, though Likir understood, as he'd brought something for Emily from the Cu'zod government.

Had the trapped creatures been traveling and waylaid during their journey to serve in an equal task to Likir?

Likir leaped, using his tail braced on the floor as leverage. Snapping his arm out, he latched onto the circular device with a claw. As he dropped back to the tiled floor, he ripped off the outer part of the container.

He expected tiny creatures to tumble out and give thanks before scampering away to freedom.

Instead, he only found wires. Blinking slowly, he frowned.

"Oh," Emily said. Her swallow took a long time going down. "That's, um…"

Derrick peered up at the device a long while. "Yeah, I see your point there, Likir. Bah humbug, right?" Laughter burst out of him, and he slapped Likir's shoulder.

Emily chuckled, though weakly. She stroked Alfred's head. The tiny beastie stared up at the ceiling then his gaze met Likir's with what Likir saw as approval.

He might not be able to see the creatures he'd freed, but they'd stopped chirping, suggesting they'd fled. All was good, now. He felt pleased to have given them this gift.

"I swear, they start playing those damn things before Halloween," Derrick said. "I get sick of listening to them, too."

He slapped Emily's arm, and she stumbled forward, tripping over the leg of a short table.

Likir caught her before she fell.

His growl ripped through the room, and his glare pinned Derrick in place.

"Oh, sorry." Reeling back, Derrick lifted his hands. "Sometimes, I just don't know my own strength." He flexed one of his upper arms, making a gesture Likir couldn't decipher.

"Thank you," Emily said softly to Likir, her voice sending more odd tingles through his chest. Her fingers cupped Alfred's head, though Alfred strained, trying to reach Likir.

Stepping back, she wiped her hands on her pants. "Okay, then. Goodbye, Derrick. If you'll follow me, Likir?" She waved to the door. "I have to get Alfred home."

Likir studied her, trying to determine where the odd tingles came from. If he didn't know better, he'd think...

A tickling sensation traveled around his wrist, and he lifted it, marveling at the pattern appearing on his scaled skin.

"Oh, huh," Emily said, turned back. "Is that a tattoo?"

"You didn't have that a minute ago, did you?" Derrick asked, moving closer. He hit his forehead, making Likir wonder how these smacking gestures could be considered friendly. "Of course you did. It's not like you stepped out to get a tat already, though it's something you should consider as it would look awesome with your scales." He peeled back his sleeve, revealing swirling patterns dancing across his skin. "I've got a sleeve."

"That's really cool," Emily said. "Are you ready, Likir?"

"I am."

The tingles spreading across his scales suggested it, but the mark on his wrist proved it.

He couldn't wrench his gaze away from Emily.

She was attractive, but all the other females he'd met were appealing in one way or another. Yet with her hair the color of ripe plugeons, a pinkish-gold that rivaled the setting sun, plus her pert nose, tiny chin, and generous lips, there was something about her he'd seen in no other. Her features and form came together in a way that made him want to step forward. Hold her.

Claim her.

This would not do. She was his host here on Earth. She would employ him and help him get settled. Guide him if he had questions or concerns during his first few months on the planet.

He should not touch her with sexual interest.

But...

Emily was his fated mate.

3

Emily

"This... This..." Likir sat in the passenger seat of Emily's Subaru, clutching the oh shit handle, while she drove away from the spaceport.

Alfred sat on his lap, where he insisted he needed to be, instead of inside his crate on the back seat. Tongue hanging out, Alfred had propped his front legs on the dash. He stared out the window, his bright gaze taking in everything they passed. His wounded paw hadn't bled again, thankfully, and it didn't seem to bother him a bit.

Her hip? Well, it was getting better.

"This...device travels too fast," Likir said, strain making his voice croaky.

"I'm only going thirty-five." But Emily slowed the vehicle to thirty.

"Please, no thirty-five." He cupped his big hands around Alfred as if he feared the small dog would suddenly be projected through the windshield.

"I'll slow down some more." Though... She was already going fifteen miles per hour below the speed limit.

A horn blared behind her and the pickup riding her

Subaru's tail whipped around her vehicle. As the guy passed them, the horn jarred again.

Alfred jumped and snarled at the pickup.

Likir jumped, too. "That… That…"

"You haven't ridden in a car before," Emily said. She eased her Subaru into the breakdown lane and parked by the curb.

A woman pushing a stroller past on the sidewalk did a doubletake when she saw Likir sitting in Emily's passenger seat. She stopped, her jaw dropping. The toddler in the stroller peered up at his mom, probably wondering why the ride had come to a halt.

Despite over four hundred Cu'zods settling on Earth over the past year, many people had still never seen an alien before other than on TV.

Likir was blue. He had scales, horns, and no hair. One-inch fangs dropped below his plump, pale blue lower lip. Plus, an intriguing row of short spikes started at his forehead and zipped up the middle of his head and down his spine. Emily presumed the spikes continued to the base of his smooth, lightly scaled tail that flicked back and forth by his shoulder. It had a forked tip, something Emily hadn't heard of but found intriguing for whatever reason. Could he grasp things with it like a hand?

If Emily hadn't seen photos of Cu'zods, she'd be shocked herself.

She'd speculated about what it would be like having an alien living and working with her. But when she heard about the sponsorship program where employers could host one of the Cu'zod settlers and help them transition into regular citizens of Earth, she knew it was something she had to do.

"Why does she peer in this direction?" Likir asked, staring at the woman with the stroller.

Emily's gaze met the woman's, and she lifted her eyebrows. *Go,* she thought. *Find someone else to stare at.*

The woman dragged her gaze from Likir and scooted forward, down the sidewalk, the toddler bouncing in his seat from the pace.

"She's curious, I guess," Emily said. "I want to explain a little about my car. Maybe then, you'll feel more comfortable riding in it." If thirty-five miles per hour startled him, she worried how he'd feel if she drove the vehicle onto the highway.

"I have personally flown starships much larger than this," he said, some of his oomph restored now that the vehicle wasn't moving.

"I plan to teach you to drive my car, though not right away." She looked around. "First, there's an engine under the hood. The vehicle is controlled with gasoline."

His nose scrunched. "Fossil fuels."

"We have electric cars, but they're expensive." It was all she could do to afford the payment on her used Subaru. She only "splurged" on an SUV because the weather in southeastern Maine could be treacherous, plus she needed the back to hold animal crates. A small car wouldn't do.

"Money is a new concept for me," he said, turning in his seat to face her. "We barter for everything we need on Cu'zod."

"Here, money rules, and you'll need it to buy food, housing, and… Not shampoo, I suppose." Remembering how often her parents had chosen to put earning money before her made her stiffen her spine. "I'm going to help you understand how everything works here on Earth."

"Thank you. I appreciate you sponsoring my settlement. When we arrive at your dwelling, I have a small gift for you from the Cu'zod royal family."

"Oh." Heat filled her face. "You don't need to give me

anything. You're here to work, right? While I'll pay you for your time, you're still going to be a great help with my business."

Where the hell was she going to find the money to pay him and help him find an apartment? With Bradley's grant and a tight budget, she could afford it, but that money would dry up in two weeks. Her belly churned as a knot of anxiety formed inside it.

"No, I insist," he said. "It is a small thing."

She wasn't sure she felt comfortable taking anything from him, but she'd wait to see what he gave her. It was common in some Earth cultures to give a host family a gift, and she wouldn't deny him if it was the same on Cu'zod.

"Back to the car." Her fingers tightened on the steering wheel. "When we drive, we're in complete control." Mostly. She wouldn't bring up accidents yet. Or slippery roads. Or pedestrians walking in front of a vehicle. "We engage the transmission in the drive gear, and when we give the car gasoline, it moves forward. We control the direction of the car with this." She tapped the wheel.

"How does one stop this...thing?"

"It's a Subaru, and we stop it with the brake, the pad to the left of the gas pedal." She pointed and he leaned over her lap, peering in that direction. "You could kinda call them go-stop pedals."

He frowned but then his face cleared as he settled back in his seat. "I would like to pilot this craft."

"Sure, but not now. I'll take you to the high school parking lot after Christmas and let you take 'er for a spin."

"I do not believe spinning is a wise thing to do with a boo-roo, but we shall see."

"Perfect." Holding back her snicker, she started the vehicle again. "I'm going to continue driving, and I'll go slow. Try to relax and trust that nothing about this ride will harm you."

"I am not worried about you harming me. I do worry about the boo-roo causing distress."

"It's an inanimate object. Look, you flew here in a ship, right?"

"I did."

"Pretend this is a ship that's flying along the ground."

"Ah. Yes." While one hand secured Alfred, his other hand tightened on the side of the seat, his claws digging in. Her vehicle was old. Dogs had puked on that seat, though she regularly used an industrial carpet shampooer on the fabric.

Still, no one had clawed their way through. Well, not yet. Today? She'd check out the situation once she'd reached her home.

"Here we go," she said, looking over her shoulder and easing back out onto the road. She let the vehicle coast at about twenty-five until they reached the stop sign. "How are you doing, there?"

"I am well, thank you," he said tightly.

A glance showed his fingers gripping the seat so tightly, they were a lighter blue than the rest of his exposed… Not skin. Flesh sounded mangy. Fine, smooth scales? That was it. She'd heard Cu'zods lived beneath the water, but he didn't appear to have gills. Had they evolved to the point they no longer needed them?

She turned the vehicle right and traveled across town while Likir stared wide-eyed out the windshield, his fingers never loosening on the seat cushion.

Alfred hopped around on Likir's lap, jumping up periodically to lick Likir's chin.

Emily had never seen anything like it. She'd resigned

herself to the idea that Alfred would live out his days with her, never loving another but her.

"Still okay?" she asked.

"I am," he gritted out. He flashed her a smile, and she realized his fangs were kind of cute. So was he, in a different way than what she found attractive in Earth men.

She turned the vehicle onto her road, gliding past the other homes, and pulled it into her driveway.

"Ugh," she said as she stared forward though the windshield. Sunlight slaked through the sky and made the snowbanks sparkle, but the world dulled when she caught sight of *him* standing on her doorstep.

"What is this…ugh?" Likir asked, glancing her way. "Is the boo-roo misbehaving?"

Okay, so boo-roo misbehaving cheered her up—somewhat. "Nope, my car's fine. As for the ugh? It's nothing." She bit back a sigh. "Absolutely nothing."

Bradley waited on her front step. Bridget was not draped all over him this time, but she could be sitting in his car, awaiting the urge for draping.

Alfred propped his front legs on the door and growled out the window.

"Could you…" Emily groaned and raked her fingers through her hair.

Likir turned toward her. "What do you need?" He braced Alfred's chest and frowned in Bradley's direction.

"Would you mind waiting here a few minutes? I need to take care of the trash."

Likir blinked slowly. "What trash?"

"Ex trash." She forced a smile. "I promise I won't be long. I'll come back to the car and get you once I've booted it to the curb."

"All right." He nodded slowly, and she could tell he didn't understand. Would she explain? Maybe.

She unbuckled, and he watched how she did it before doing the same. But he remained in the car as she skidded up her slippery walk and halted at the base of her front steps. She didn't like giving Bradley the edge with his height, but the stoop was shallow. There wasn't room for both of them to stand on the landing, and she had no urge for draping.

"There you are," Bradley said, staring down his nose at her.

"Yes. This is my house, as you may remember. Where else would I be?" She stiffened her upper lip. "Why are you here, Bradley? We have nothing more to say to each other." She crossed her arms on her chest and tapped her foot on the snowy ground.

"That's not a polite way to treat someone who gave you a two-week extension on your grant," Bradley said. "Your current behavior makes me wonder if I should reconsider."

A chill sunk into her, and it wasn't from the frosty air. But really, two weeks wouldn't make much difference. She was sunk unless she could find another source of ongoing funding.

"And here I was, about to offer you and your fictious boyfriend two invitations to the Christmas Costume Ball," Bradley said, patting his right chest with his leather glove. His burly black coat shifted across his upper thighs.

"The ball is sold out. There are no more tickets." She'd tried to get one months ago. Everyone who was somebody in town would attend this event. If she could attend, she'd have a chance to solicit funding for *Grannie's Rescue* that would take her well beyond the paltry grant Bradley had reluctantly offered. Alcohol and open purses often went together.

Bradley dangled two pieces of thick, embossed card

decorated with holly and berries near Emily's nose. "If you're nice, I'll give these to you. But..." His chuckle rivaled that of a Disney villain. "Tell you what. I'll give them to you if you introduce me to your supposed date."

Her growl rose up her throat. "What game are you playing this time, Bradley? Spit it out."

"I'm calling your bet," he said. "I have two tickets to the Ball, and I'll give them to you if you can produce a boyfriend. The one you said you had earlier, remember?" He peered around her. "I don't see anyone here, so perhaps you were just joking around earlier?"

"Don't be an ass. You came here to taunt me, and I won't put up with it."

"I tell you what," he said with an evil grin. "Give me your boyfriend's name, then, and I'll give you the tickets. I *will* expect to meet him at the Ball, however, as Bridget and I will be there, too."

"I *do* have a boyfriend," she blurted out. The words had erupted from her before she could keep them inside. What was she going to do? What was she going to do?!

Mortification filled her. Bradley would not let this go. He'd press and press until she crumbled and admitted she wasn't dating anyone. Then she'd turn into Cinderella on the night of the ball, sitting home alone when she could be schmoozing with potential doners. "My boyfriend's name?" She swallowed, but the lump of dismay wouldn't go down. Her throat ached, and her eyes stung with bitter tears. "It's... It's..."

"Allow me to introduce myself," a male said in a deep, smooth voice behind her. Likir placed his arm around Emily's shoulders and kissed her on the cheek. Alfred nestled in his other arm, glaring at Bradley. "I am Likir Hidaell Drukvals Thuzok." He nodded at her ex while Bradley gaped. "I am Emily's friendly boy."

Likir

The snarly male's gaze slammed into Likir. "Emily? You're dating this scaled alien creature?"

"I am a Cu'zod warrior," Likir said stiffly. He carefully lowered Alfred onto the walkway and reached for the bag he'd dropped to the ground. An insult like this would be returned in warrior fashion.

Emily stilled his arm. She leaned in close, shielding her mouth from the nasty male. "Thank you. You're a godsend. I promise I'll explain everything once we get inside." Lifting Alfred into her arms, she straightened and flicked her hand toward the irritating male. "This is Bradley. Bradley? Likir. My, um…Likir."

Little did she know he *was* her Likir. The mate symbol on his wrist proved it. He hadn't had a moment to think about what this meant. Seeing and then hearing this unpleasant male berating Emily had been too much for Likir to stand for. He'd left the car with Alfred, prepared to rush to her defense.

"Surely this *creature* isn't your boyfriend?" Brad-lee

sputtered, staring down his nose at Likir, which wasn't simple to do as Likir equaled this annoying male in height despite him standing on the ground and Brad-lee, the top step.

"You guessed it." Emily jumped up. She snatched two slips of paper from Brad-lee's hand and pocketed them. "Game. Match. Set. As you can see, I've got a date for the ball, meat cheeks. Thanks for the tickets."

Likir savored the irritation blooming on evil Brad-lee's face, as well as what Likir assumed was a slur. "Yes, meat cheeks," Likir mimicked. "Thank you." He didn't know what the ball was, let alone meat cheeks, and he didn't care. Seeing the relief and happiness on Emily's face was enough for him.

Likir flashed his fangs, though he made sure he imparted a subtle threat in the movement when he directed it at Brad-lee. It was clear Emily was upset with this angry male, and if she was, so was Likir.

"He appears hostile," Likir told Emily. "I know how to handle unruly beings." Undoing the fastening on the top of his bag, he slid his sword from its sheath and swiped it through the air, whistling it past Brad-lee's chin. "Would you like me to skewer him, Emily?"

Emily's snort turned into full laughter.

Likir joined in, savoring the sound of her happiness.

Alfred yipped and wiggled in her arms.

"I, er…" Brad-lee's face lost its color. He reeled to the side and skidded off the top step, nearly losing his footing when one shoe shot out from beneath him on the walkway. "I have to go pick up Bridget."

He skidded around Likir, entangling himself in the shrubbery planted to the side of the steps. Small red balls dangling from the branches swayed.

On the same level, this puny Earthling male only came

to Likir's shoulder. Brad-lee must drink considerable Coo-coo Coola.

"Come back," Likir called to Brad-lee as he slipped and slid down the path toward his vehicle.

Brad-lee peered over his shoulder. When he saw Likir striding toward him, he barked and started to run. His feet went out from underneath him, and he landed on the path on his ass. Cursing, he rose and rushed to a black vehicle sitting on the side of the street in front of the dwelling.

"I almost *would* like you to stab him," Emily said, coming over to stand beside Likir. In her arms, Alfred barked as if swearing at Brad-lee.

She wiped her eyes and peered up at Likir through spiky eyelashes, making him realize all over again how appealing this female was.

His true mate.

What was he going to do about this? He'd learned Earthlings did not mate like Cu'zods. They did a thing called dating before choosing to join with another. By stating he was her friendly boy, had he initiated the Earthling dating rituals? He needed to study the literature he'd received before leaving Cu'zod, something he'd yet to make time for other than giving it a cursory glance.

Brad-lee's vehicle started and roared away faster than some space cruisers.

"He is not going thirty-five," Likir pointed out.

"Nope." She chuckled and returned to the front of her dwelling, where she inserted a slender metal device into a round panel on the door.

He grabbed his bag on the way past, securing his sword inside again, then climbed the steps to join her.

She opened the door and waved for him to enter the dwelling ahead of her. "Welcome to my home, Likir. I hope you'll be happy here. It's not much, but my grannie left it to me free and clear." Shadows filled her face. "I hope I can keep it that way."

He wasn't sure what she meant by free and clear or keeping it that way, but he did wish to set aside her sadness. He was grateful he'd made her laugh about Brad-lee.

"I hope I did not intrude by offering to be your friendly boy," he said as he lowered his bag onto the floor in the entryway.

"I appreciate it. I'm embarrassed, actually." Nuzzling the top of Alfred's head with her chin, she watched Likir.

"Why?"

"Because you just got here, and then you were forced to jump in and play my hero."

"Hero?"

"You did an honorable thing and pulled me out of a tough situation." After placing Alfred on the floor, she pulled the slips of paper from her pocket and held them up over her head, swinging her hips back and forth. "But it worked. I did it. *We* did it! Two tickets to the Christmas Costume Ball, where I can lure a few of the guests into opening their wallets and saving my business!" She twirled around, her arms over her head, but stumbled when Alfred hopped around her, barking with joy.

Likir's arms snapped out to right her before she fell.

She peered up at him from within his embrace. "You're quick on your feet, Likir. Quick with words, too." Easing out of his arms, she tucked the papers back inside her pocket.

"Explain what this friendly boy activity means?" he asked.

"Because you stepped up to play my hero, Bradley now thinks you and I are dating."

Ah, so Likir was correct. Extending the offer to be a friendly boy was part of Earthling dating protocol.

Wait. *Think* they were dating.

"This is not real," he said with a touch of sadness. "You wish for a *pretend* friendly boy to dissuade the other male."

"Bradley's my ex," she said, her lips souring.

"A letter of your alphee-bet?"

Shaking her head, she took his coat and placed it on a hook near the door, adding her own beside it. His was comically huge compared to hers. After taking measurements, the Earthlings made clothing for each Cu'zod. They were waiting when he arrived at the spaceport.

"Bradley is my ex, which means former boyfriend," she said. A click, and she lifted a strap over her shoulders, releasing the Alfred bag from her chest. She lowered it onto a table near the door.

Alfred scooted over to Likir surprisingly fast on his three feet and proceeded to sniff Likir's footwear.

"I can see why Brad-lee is an X," Likir said. "He is not friendly enough to be your boy."

Emily's grin was gone too fast for Likir to savor it.

"He sure isn't." Sucking in a deep breath, she released it. "I have a huge favor to ask of you, and it's going to make me squirm, but…you kinda already put yourself into this position."

He wasn't sure how her squirming played into this, but he was curious to find out what she needed. "Yes?"

"Could you continue to pretend to be my boyfriend until after the ball? It's on Christmas eve, in six days. If I know Bradley, he won't let this go. He'll be determined to prove our relationship isn't real. If he suspects we're faking it, he'll find a way to take the tickets back."

Likir dipped forward in a short bow. "I will be happy to

be your friendly boy." No, that wasn't right. His damn translator. "*Boyfriend*, that is, for as long as you have need."

"Thank you. After the ball, we can pretend we broke up, and you'll be free to go out with whomever you want." She smiled wanly.

"I do not know anyone on Earth I wish to do the dating with." Except her. He shouldn't feel sad that this was pretend. He did need to learn how beings mated on Earth. He wanted to fit in. But what if he didn't want to be free from her? She was his fated mate and offered him the chance to step into the role he already desired.

A true mating did not compel a Cu'zod male to be with his mate, but Likir liked Emily already. He desired her. And with Cu'zods mating with Earthlings, he had to admit he'd already started to dream of he and Emily doing the same after they'd gotten to know each other. It was much too soon for emotions, however. They'd just met.

It was important he follow Earth mate-obtaining customs. Dating was just one activity he'd expected to try when he arrived here. Why not with Emily?

Tonight, he would use the Earthling inter-nest with the device Derrick gave him, called a phoon. Surely there were details about dating in the inter-nest he could employ with Emily.

Perhaps they could turn fake dating into something real.

"Alfred," she said, tapping her thigh. "Leave the poor guy's feet alone."

Alfred had climbed onto Likir's footwear and sat, staring up him.

"I do not mind him here. He is a good…" He wasn't exactly sure what to call the Alfred creature.

"Dog. Or doggie, if you want to be cute."

What was this cute and did he wish to discover it? Another thing to investigate on the inter-nest.

She bent down and coaxed Alfred away from Likir by rubbing her fingertips together and speaking in a high-pitched voice. "Come on, little guy. You can ride with me."

Alfred peered from her hand to Likir, then whined. His front paws lifted onto Likir's legs.

"What does he need?" Likir asked.

"He wants you to pick him up, but you don't have to."

"I do not mind." Lifting the doo-gee, he held the creature against his chest. Alfred sniffed then stretched his neck up. His short, pink tongue glided across Likir's chin, making him shiver in a pleasant way. "What is this gesture Alfred makes? He did it in the boo-roo."

"It's his way of showing you he likes you," Emily said, frowning.

Liking was a good thing, correct? Why did she frown?

"It's just…" She shook her head, and her reddish-gold hair bounced around her face.

Hair was such a wonderous thing. He also wondered about skin. *Emily's* skin, actually. What would it feel like beneath his fingertips? How would she respond if he touched her?

Thoughts he needed to dismiss since they were faking a relationship.

Emily held out her arms to the doo-gee. "Are you sure you don't want me to take him?"

"I like this…Alfred."

She nodded slowly. "It's a miracle, actually. He's never taken to anyone other than me. You'll soon learn about your job here, and my business. Alfred is one example. I rescue animals no one else wants then find them forever homes."

"Alfred will find a forever home?"

"I don't think it's possible for this little fella." She came close enough Likir could catch her scent in the air. Light, slightly floral, plus containing something he couldn't define.

Emily. It was solely her. He liked it very much.

"Alfred may remain with me until we find his forever home," Likir said.

She chuckled. "Well, he can stay with you until bedtime. He's pretty particular about who he sleeps with." Her hand flicked out toward the dwelling in general as she turned. "Let me give you a quick tour, and then I'll show you your room, and you can get settled." She nudged her chin toward the stairs. "Upstairs, there are two bedrooms, plus a bathroom we'll share. Downstairs... Well, let me show you."

Striding around him, she stepped into the adjacent living quarters holding a small couch, two chairs that would feel cramped if he sat in them, and a flat box mounted on the wall that must be the tree-vee. He'd heard about tree-vees during his lessons on the way to this planet. No, wait. *Tee-vee.*

"Feel welcome to watch any movie you'd like," she said, glancing at the tee-vee. "I have Netflix and a bunch of DVDs."

"Thank you." He followed her across the room and into the adjacent eating area.

"My kitchen," she said. She opened a white box, the refridge, if he remembered correctly. "When we go grocery shopping, you can pick out some things you'd like to eat, and we can store the cold items here." Easing around a table with four chairs, she approached the cabinets. "I've cleaned out two of these for you to keep whatever else you'd like to buy, the things that don't need refrigeration. I'll, of course, pay for those expenses as room and board is included in the sponsorship agreement."

Empty shelves awaited his purchases, but he couldn't imagine what he would buy. "I have heard of these places where you purchase food items, and I cannot wait to see them. On Cu'zod, we barter for what we need. We have no currency. And we use replicators to prepare our food. Long ago, we hunted beneath the sea and sometimes on our small landmasses, but we no longer need to."

"I think Cu'zod sounds amazing. I can't imagine it but hope to see photos someday."

"I will be happy to answer any questions you might have."

"Thank you." She smiled at Alfred bouncing around her. Truly, this doo-gee was full of energy. "We buy things here rather than fabricate them. Wait until you check out the department store. It's going to blow your mind."

"I hope it does not." He made a note to himself to avoid department stores if they brought about exploding brains.

Her fingers stilled on the cabinet door, and her lower lip twitched. "Blow your mind means you'll be amazed."

"Oh, yes, of course. I welcome having my mind blown, then."

She chuckled. "You're funny."

"Thank you?" What had he said that was humorous? He swore, his translator messed up half of what either of them said. But they'd figure this out eventually.

She gestured to a door along one wall. "That leads to the animal areas, but as it's getting late, let's stick with the main house for now." Continuing into a hallway, she opened a door on the right. "This is the downstairs bathroom. We'll share the one upstairs."

"One bathes here." He'd also read about these rooms and couldn't wait to test each object in the tiny room.

"Here or upstairs." She closed the door and opened another farther down the hall. "This is my office. I've set up a desk for you, but…" Her gaze spanned his taller frame. "I had measurements, but reality is proving a challenge. I'm worried your chair won't be big enough for you."

"I will manage."

"You're right. We'll figure something out." She paused and leaned against the wall. "When I signed up for this, I had no idea what I was getting into. I saw it as a chance to welcome someone to Earth and help them settle. But I like you, Likir. You're funny, and I think we're going to get along well." She rubbed Alfred's ears. "If this little guy is anything to go by, my animal friends are going to be eager to get to know you, as well."

Alfred squirmed in her arms, and she lowered the little beastie to the floor.

"Is three legs the usual for doo-gees?" he asked, following her out to the entrance area.

"For Alfred, it is," she said as she started up the stairs. Alfred followed her, turning to watch Likir lift his bag and hook it over his shoulder. "When he was rescued, he was in pretty sad shape," she said. "But a kind vet and my love has helped him come a long way already. If someone doesn't want to adopt him, I'll keep him myself."

"Someone removed one of his legs?" Likir asked as he followed her up the stairs.

She paused on the landing covered with a thick fabric that squished beneath Likir's footwear. The floor of the living quarters downstairs was coated with the same material, and he wasn't sure what to make of it.

Tears shimmered in Emily's eyes. "His former owners

hurt Alfred, but he knows I won't let anything bad happen to him again. It's hard to trust others, as I well know." Her eyes closed briefly before reopening. "Life can be tough for both people and animals."

A fierce feeling of protectiveness filled Likir, and he pressed his fist to his chest. "I, too, will defend Alfred." He dipped his head forward. "You, as well."

5

Emily

Emily led Likir to the guest room that she'd recently claimed as her own until they got him settled in his own apartment. The guest room had a queen bed while the master suite had a California king.

When she heard Cu'zods were over seven-feet-tall, she was presented with a dilemma. It wouldn't be fair for her to take the big bed while he slept with his feet hanging off the bottom of the queen. As it was, his feet might still dangle over the end of the king.

She opened the door, filling the hall with late-day sunlight. "This is my room."

Easing around him, she paused and looked up, up, up. When he held Alfred in the car and downstairs, treating the pup with infinite gentleness, Emily's heart split wide open. It was easy to like someone who'd treat someone smaller than them with kindness, but it was more than that.

Alfred, her gruff, wounded old man doggo, had sought out Likir. He'd never done that with another person before. If anything, he barked, tried to nip, or hid behind her legs.

She wasn't sure what to make of his growing affection for her sad pet.

"I, um..." Their bodies brushed together as they moved into the room. Clothing brushed, that is. This wasn't skin on scales.

She wondered what that would feel like.

It was dangerous to allow herself to feel attraction for Likir, especially when she'd already insisted they were only pretending.

The warmth of his body against hers didn't feel like pretend. Neither did the sudden heat flooding her limbs. It centered in her core, making her feel like collapsing on the bed. He'd follow, his mouth...

Earth to Emily: wake up!

"I'm sorry," she said, scooting past him and hurrying back into the hall and to the bathroom between the two rooms. She opened the door.

"Why are you sorry?" he asked, following.

"Oh, um, nothing."

He frowned, and she couldn't stop studying his lips that were much like a human's only a paler blue than his scales.

His tail looped around and teased along her ankle

She shivered and tried to shrug off the growing need she felt for Likir.

"This is the bathroom," she croaked.

It might be time to hide out in her office until she regained control of her wayward libido. Likir had agreed to pretend to be her boyfriend.

Fake boyfriends did not come with benefits.

"And your room is down here," she said, leading him in that direction. She needed to forget how good he smelled, like a spice she'd longed for all her life but never tasted.

Opening the door, she stepped inside the larger room. "I've given you this room because the bed's bigger."

"You mean, this is yours," he said, and she wondered how he knew. She'd moved all her personal items to the other bedroom days ago.

"It was but it's yours now."

"Thank you. It...smells of you."

Ugh, body odor?

Probably not stink, since his flashed smile suggested he found her scent as intriguing as she did his.

Stop that, right now, she chided herself.

"There are spare blankets in the closet, and I left a few towels for you on the chair. For showering. I'll explain the bathroom fixtures to you... Well, I probably should explain them now since you might need to use the toilet." Ducking around him, she returned to the bathroom. "This is it." She demonstrated flushing and told him how to use the fixture.

"How does this urine collector function?" he asked with a frown, leaning over the white porcelain device.

"Something about water pressure," she said with a scrunch of her face. "I'm not really sure." Lifting the lid off the back, she revealed the toilet guts. "All I know is that this stuff makes it happen."

He stared into the water chamber a long time. "Amazing."

Only Likir would find a toilet amazing.

"Do you have something like this on Cu'zod?" she asked, curious about how they went to the bathroom. She knew the physical mechanics were the same, but did they pee into a toilet like here on Earth?

"We have devices such as this, though they do not appear the same."

The bathroom was small. And he still smelled great. She wanted to lean against him, close her eyes, and suck him all in. Imprint him on her mind.

Totally shouldn't do something like that.

His nostrils flared. "You…" A frown took over his face, making his scaled brow ridges scrunch, and he lifted his hand up, displaying the etched, dark blue band of tiny leaves encircling his wrist she'd seen at the spaceport. "This…too-too. Do you know what it means for a Cu'zod?"

She shook her head. It couldn't be a real tattoo. He hadn't been here long enough to get one. Unless tattoos were common on Cu'zod. But she swore he hadn't had the marking when she first met him at the spaceport.

Something flitted through her mind… She'd heard of a symbol like this but couldn't remember where.

"It means my true mate is with me," he said in a deep, husky voice. He watched her face as if he expected…something. She couldn't imagine what.

"Where, um…is she?"

Damn, he had a true mate? Just her luck being sorta interested in more than just friends with Likir and he announces some other woman is his fated mate.

"You," he said, his slitted, reptilian green eyes penetrated hers. "It means *you* are my true mate, Emily."

6

Likir

He didn't expect Emily to swoon in his arms. Or kiss him. But he also didn't expect her to deny their growing bond.

"That's not possible," she said, her fingers tracing her trembling lower lip. He wanted to taste it, suck it into his mouth. Replace her fingers with his tongue.

His tail coiled around her leg, seeking upward. Tails were bolder than Likir dared to behave.

"I realize this is sudden," he said.

Her breath snorted out. "Yup."

"And we barely know each other."

"Yup, again."

"But the markings do not lie."

Her fingers fluttered at her throat. He took her hands in his and clasped them between his palms, stilling their tremble.

"Tell me what is expected from a friendly boy—boyfriend," he said, leaning closer to her.

If he closed his eyes, he could drink in her scent. If he

kept his eyes open, he could read her every reaction on her face. Either was equally appealing.

"Oh, we won't have to do much. It'll mostly matter at the ball and if we happen to run into him before then. I don't want Bradley calling me out for lying. If he suspects this is pretend, he'll take the tickets back."

"I will escort you to this ball?"

"Yes," she said, seemingly as mesmerized by him as he was with her. She leaned closer, and their bodies brushed together. When it happened inside her room, his cock twitched. The blinder nubs at the top and bottom of his cock started vibrating. "We, um, will need to convince him we're really together."

"I assume this is best done with a display of intimacy?"

"Probably." Her gaze fell to his mouth, and he so much wanted to ask her what she was feeling. "We might need to…practice."

Unable to resist her lure, his arm teased around the back of her waist. He waited for her to tug away.

She pressed herself fully against him.

"I believe you are correct," he said, heat blazing inside him. They'd only recently met, but he wanted her. Needed her. "If we practice, it will feel seamless."

"Then we, um, probably should do it, don't you think?" Her gaze never moved away from his mouth.

He lifted her chin with his thumb claw and lowered his mouth above hers. One taste. That was all he needed. He would be satisfied—for now—with that.

His lips brushed hers, and her gasp slipped between them, warming him up further. "Like this? Would a gesture like this convince Bradley?" He swallowed through a throat tight with burgeoning emotion. It was forbidden. This was supposed to be pretend.

It didn't feel like pretend.

Her mouth quirked up on one side, and her eyes sparkled. "I'm not sure if that would be enough to convince anyone."

A dare rang out in her voice, and Likir had never backed down from a challenge.

"Ah," he said. He tugged her fully against him, showing her his need. "Perhaps this would convince the nasty x-male that you are already taken."

His mouth claimed hers, gently at first then with growing heat.

Moaning, she pressed herself against him.

He was desperate to feel everything, eager to take all she'd give. His tongue glided inside her mouth, meeting hers, and they entwined.

A raging need possessed him, channeling to his groin. He was big, and his mate was tiny and precious. He would need to take care not to hurt her.

Her fingertips slid beneath his shirt, gliding across his scales. She moaned, and he deepened his kiss.

His tail teased up her inner thigh. Humans had no tails, and he wasn't sure how she'd respond to the touch of his. The forked tip flickered against the stiff material encasing her legs.

She widened her stance, and he stroked across the juncture between her thighs.

Tipping her head back, she groaned as his tail continued to press against her.

If only they were naked.

Lying on the floor.

Him over her, his cock poised at her hot, wet opening.

A raging fever took hold of him, and he tugged her closer, engulfing her with his arms.

Panting, she pressed her body against his tail while it rubbed her.

He wanted to shred her clothing with his claws. His own, too. And then he'd—

One moment. What was he doing? This was a tease. A sample.

Pretend. A kiss they were practicing in case they needed to show nasty Brad-lee that Emily was truly, completely taken.

She didn't know yet what a true mating was, and Likir needed to remain patient until her feelings grew to match his own.

When she pulled away and backed into one of the white, shiny fixtures, Likir watched her with hooded eyes.

She traced her lips with a finger, and her high color suggested she wanted more, too.

Pushing when this was so new would be unwise. He was in this for more than a few kisses. More than letting his tail taste her body. Despite how sudden it was, he wanted it all.

His inflamed cock surged against his pants, eager to be free. Eager to delve deep inside her.

But this was pretend.

Maybe.

"I think that will…" She sucked in a deep breath and released it. "Wow."

"Wow?" Was this a good thing, this wow?

"That was…" Shuffling to the door, she pulled it open with trembling fingers. "I think that will convince Bradley. Hell, that kiss would convince the entire world."

He wanted to tease her, to suggest they needed more practice, but he could see she was unsettled. The idea of being a true mate was easier for him to understand and accept since this was a big part of his culture. He carried the symbol proving she was his.

Earthlings used dating to determine if they wished to mate, and this was what Likir needed to do.

Once he'd searched the inter-nest to find out how dating was conducted, he'd make a plan, because he did not wish to give up his little Earthling female now that he'd found her.

His groin still on fire, and his cock a thick, aching rod in his pants, he followed her out into the hall.

"I have some things to do downstairs," she said, running all ten of her fingers through her hair. She then raked her hands down her face. "You can unpack if you'd like. Get settled into your room. I'll start dinner and it'll be ready in twenty minutes or so?" Her attention drifted to where his cock nudged against his pants, and she gulped.

"I will join you in twenty minutes or so, then."

"Okay, um, good." She fled, scooping up Alfred and racing down the stairs.

He walked to his room, but it didn't take him long to unpack.

Other than some ceremonial gear and comfortable items, he'd brought very little clothing after being told everything would be provided for him by this planet's government. They'd gifted him with five pairs of pants; an equal number of shirts with both long and short sleeves; the coat downstairs and a lighter version of the same; three pairs of footwear; and stretchy narrow tubes he assumed would fit over his feet.

Standing back, he held up the even stranger garment he found in the bag Derrick gave him. A bit like pants, they were thinner and had very short legs. An opening in the front almost appeared to be designed...

No, it could not be, could it?

He held it against his groin and could see it would fit over this area, but why would he need a cock-viewing garment? The hole was placed in the right area so he could reach inside and pull out his cock if he wished to show it to someone. Did Earthlings do this in social situations? It couldn't be.

This made no sense. Derrick had not been wearing anything like this.

However, it was cold outside. A flimsy cock-viewing garment such as this would be inappropriate in the current climate.

Perhaps Likir was supposed to wear this when it was hot, which he heard happened in this region of Earth during the summer months.

So odd, but one must do what the local customs dictated. He would set aside the cock-viewing garment and would pull it out when it was warmer.

Sitting on the side of the bed, he lifted the phoon Derrick gave him and entered the inter-nest as Derrick had shown him.

Likir had practiced Earth writing while traveling from Cu'zod, and he laboriously ticked the correct letters for Earth dating techniques. Many options blasted onto the viewbox, and he studied a few, soon feeling overwhelmed.

Flowers. Prom proposals—what were those? Long walks and picnics—another unfamiliar term.

Some of the options on the viewbox took him to other screens where faces smiled at him, and something flashed asking him to *Sign Up for Hot Dates!*

More confused than when he started, Likir dropped the phoon on his bed. This inter-nest was confusing.

Dating was confusing

Earth was confusing.

But he knew one thing: he wanted to win Emily's affection.

Perhaps he didn't need the inter-nest to do such a

thing. He could pursue her like any other Cu'zod warrior did once he found is true mate. Kisses were an excellent start.

If she asked him for pretend fucking, he would gladly cooperate with that, as well. However, he would not be able to keep his emotions in check and fuck her in a fake manner. Anyone who thought a Cu'zod male could do so would be wrong.

She was his true mate. Naturally, he would fuck her in a complete manner.

With a huff, he left his room. He located Emily in the kitchen area, stirring something in a silver pan on the stove.

"Can I help?" he asked, leaning against the doorway. He had to hunch his head forward or his horns would impact with the upper surface. How could Earthlings maneuver in such low spaces? Oh, yes, they drank much Coo-coo Coola to remain short.

"Oh, no thanks. I've got it." She flashed him a smile. "I'm making mac 'n cheese. I don't imagine you've had that before."

"I sampled a few Earthing dishes while traveling here, but that was not one of them."

"It's gooey and cheesy, and it will make your taste buds pop."

Minds blowing. Taste buds popping. Earthlings used such wonderous phrases.

"After dinner, I want to put up the tree," she said. "It doesn't feel like Christmas without one."

"Put the tree…?"

"It's a fake one, but I have an evergreen candle we can light to make the room smell like it's real. The tree was my gran's, so it's kinda a nostalgia thing for me to put it up in the house she gave me."

"Explain this Christmas to me?"

"It's a holiday," she said, telling him about the religious background related to the day. "While my gran was into that part of it, I'm more about the tree, the treats we bake, and the warm feeling this time of year gives me. I feel close to everyone, and I guess that has value, too."

"You said this was your gran's house?"

Shadows crossed Emily's face. "Yes, she died nine months ago and left it to me."

"I'm sorry for her death."

"Thanks. She was old, but I don't think anyone's old enough to die. I… I lived with her from the time I was five. My parents were busy. They worked a lot. It made sense for Grannie to take care of me and then, well, to adopt me." What he took as a fake smile rose on her face.

"You did not live with your parents?"

"They were busy," she said lightly, shifting to face the stove. She moved the silver pan over and then drained steaming water from another, into the sink. Small white blobs were caught in a straining device as she did it.

Busy? If he didn't know better, he'd believe they hadn't wanted her, but that couldn't be true. They were a family.

"Anyway," she said. "I've lived with her since I was five. When I got older, I worked as a barista and volunteered at a rescue a few towns over from here. Eventually, Grannie encouraged me to start my own rescue, using the attached buildings for my business. When she died, she left everything to me." Her voice lowered to a whisper. "I just hope I don't lose it."

He wasn't sure how she could lose a large dwelling such as this, but it was clear the thought caused her distress.

She bustled to the counter and dumped the steamy white lumps into a glass dish. Returning to the stove, she spooned a thick creamy sauce over the lumps. A few stirs and she placed the dish inside the oven.

He'd heard about ovens and mee-croo-waves, which he hoped to soon try. They didn't have anything like this on Cu'zod, having transitioned to food processing devices and replicators years ago. If a Cu'zod was hungry, he told the device what he wished to eat, and the final product was delivered within seconds. A paste made of the proper nutrients to sustain life was regularly poured into the back of the device.

No one hunted or cooked on Cu'zod any longer. Perhaps his government would share this technology with Earthlings, too, and they would stop preparing meals in this archaic manner.

"Would you feed Alfred?" she asked as she removed a white package with pictures of green lumps on the surface from the top panel of the refridge. "I'll get some broccoli going."

"What will I feed him? You have no replicator."

"There's dry food in a bag in that cupboard," she nudged her shoulder, "and a covered can of wet food on the counter. One half a scoop of dry, one tablespoon of wet, and then a splash of water. Stir it up, and he'll be all over it."

This was very interesting.

"His dish is on the floor," she added.

Likir located the bowl and set it on the counter. Dry food… Opening the cupboard, his sinuses were assaulted with a strange smell that was not exactly pleasant, but all he saw was a bag with a larger version of a doo-gee on the side. The scoop sat on the floor of the cupboard beside it. He opened the top and half-filled the measuring device, dumping it into the bowl.

"Alfred does not eat the taste bud popping meal with us?" Likir asked.

"Oh, he'd love mac 'n cheese, but it's not good for him."

"Yet we will eat it."

She grinned. "Funny."

He wasn't making a joke as far as he knew. Closing the cupboard, he sought the wet food, finding a can with another doo-gee on the side sitting on the counter. When he lifted the lid, a horrible scent filled the air. "I do not think we should feed this to Alfred."

"He loves it. Trust me." She uplifted the open white bag, and green lumps clattered into a silver pan. Holding it under the faucet, she added water then covered it and placed it on the smooth, upper stove surface.

"If you say so." He located a spoon that was not the size of a table, but Alfred was tiny. Likir doubted the doo-gee could eat a quantity of that size. After scooping out a spoonful of the brown gook, he added a bit of water and stirred it. "Should I taste it to ensure it is safe to feed Alfred?" He had a bad feeling about this. "In all honesty, I would prefer to replicate a small slice of floodor for him instead."

"We don't have replicators, and Alfred loves dog food." She took the bowl from him and placed it on the floor.

Alfred looked from the bowl to them, then back to the bowl.

"See?" Likir said. "He prefers to eat the mind-blowing food with us." Which actually smelled tasty. The aroma swirled around him, beaconing him toward the oven.

"We can give him one bite, but he has to eat his own food."

"Why?"

Alfred yipped, and Likir decided he added his own *why* to the conversation.

"It's not good for him."

Likir wasn't convinced what they were feeding Alfred was good for him, either. "I will hunt for Alfred, if that is acceptable."

She spun around, and her lips fluttered as if she was undecided about frowning or smiling. "Why and what?"

He shrugged. "Since you have no replicator, and these dry and wet substances are not appealing to Alfred, I assume he and the other creatures we care for will need meat to sustain them."

"They get that from their kibble."

Likir's scowl took in Alfred's uneaten food. "He does not enjoy this kee-ble." Puffing his chest, he stood taller, though that made his horns tap against the ceiling. If Cu'zods were going to live on Earth, they would need to build taller dwellings. "I will hunt whatever beast roams outside."

"Other than a random mouse, I think the only beast you're going to find is Santa's reindeer, and I don't recommend shooting or ripping it apart to feed the animals."

"This Santa, he is dangerous? A worthy opponent for a Cu'zod warrior?"

Her laughter snorted out. "Funny. Not at all. Come on into the living room, and I'll introduce you to Santa while the mac 'n cheese is baking."

He followed her into the living quarters—living *room*—and sat beside her on the sofa.

She tugged a book off the low glass surface in front of her and laid it on her lap. "This is a story about Santa. It's a classic."

"This Santa's story is in pictures?"

"Do you have books on Cu'zod?"

"A few, but only among the elite." His family estate actually had a small library and twenty-two books, though they were ancient tomes no one had opened in years.

"That's too bad. Here, we have lots of books. I'll teach you to read if you'd like."

"I have learned to read your language, but that is for research." For things such as dating. "I cannot see any other purpose to this reading."

"Likir," she said in a scolding tone that was negated by the sparkle in her pretty eyes, "reading is amazing. With a book, you can go anywhere."

He frowned and traced his claw down the colorful cover. "I can go anywhere I wish already."

"I suppose you can in a spaceship. But with a book, you can travel from the comfort of your own living room without ever leaving. It's a great escape." She flipped back the cover, and despite his skepticism, he was intrigued by the bright picture of a male with white fur on his face wearing a red and white suit. His cheeks were pink, indicating embarrassment, though it was unclear from the picture why.

Emily read, and he focused as much on her expressive face and lilting voice as the words she spoke.

No creatures were stirring, not even a mouse. This did not bode well for his hunting expedition to obtain alternate food for Alfred and the creatures in the rescue.

"So, this Saint Nicholas is Santa?" he asked, intrigued by this tale despite his initial skepticism.

"He is."

"He attacks dwellings by encroaching on their rooftops."

She chuckled. "He's welcome to encroach on their rooftops."

"An intruder is welcome?" He traced his finger across the page. "This makes no sense."

"It's actually a fairytale, a story for those who are young at heart who wish to believe there's magic in their lives. Nowadays, only kids believe Santa will come to their houses on Christmas eve and leave presents. Maybe we're all kids at heart at one time or another?"

"I wish to learn more about this legend the hol-ee-day of Christmas. Is there more you can share with me?"

She tilted her head, thinking, before her face cleared and she held up one finger. "You know what? I think there is. In addition to working with you here and assisting you in finding your way on Earth, I'll take you to a bunch of places to help you discover the wonders of Christmas."

Emily

*E*arly the next morning, Emily was making pumpkin chocolate chip muffins in the kitchen and contemplating what she needed to do after consuming a couple of them warm, slathered in butter.

In five more days, it would be Christmas eve, and Emily had her work cut out for her in more ways than one.

She had to find a way to fund her business for the long term. The Ball was her first place to start, though she had a few ideas she could also look into. That list of grants she hadn't had time to apply for, would be one. Standing on a street corner would be another. She was only kidding herself about the last.

She popped the muffin tin into the oven then washed the dishes while singing *Deck the Halls*… Sashaying her hips along with the tune.

What else did she need to do? Almost time for a list.

She needed to show Likir how to do his job. That would begin today, after breakfast. Once he had the routine down pat, she'd be able to focus on catching up with the piles of paperwork waiting on her desk, including those grants.

She wanted to share the magic of Christmas with him.

So many tasks, and she had to do it all while not letting her heart get involved with her new houseguest.

He'd said something about her being his mate, and hell, had that been quite the kiss, but they were still pretending, right?

She'd read about Cu'zod true mates online, but he had to be joking. Teasing. Confused.

She ruefully realized his behavior could only be attributed to the latter. He had...space lag, assuming there was such a thing.

"What is this fa-la-la-la-la?" he asked from the doorway.

She spun, nearly dropping the soapy measuring cup she held in her hand. "Oh, hi!" Heat flared in her face. "I'm not a very good singer, but the fa-la-la-la-la stuff is part of a Christmas song."

"There are songs surrounding this holiday?" He moved into the room like a big panther, sleek, muscled, and dangerous—to her heart. His tail had intrigued her from the moment she first saw it. Thick where it connected at the base, then slimming to the forked tip. Yesterday, it had stroked her between the legs and... Oh, my, she needed to stop thinking about that.

"There are tons of Christmas songs," she said. "I play them in the animal areas. By the end of the week, you'll know all the words."

He frowned, and she wasn't sure if he did so because he didn't want to learn songs, he didn't sing, or her muffins didn't smell good.

Actually, they smelled amazing, but after their conversation about dog food last night, followed by him gushing about mac 'n cheese while sneaking bites to Alfred, she wasn't sure what flavors he enjoyed most.

"I've made muffins," she said. "Would you like some coffee?" Crossing the room to the pot, she took down two cups from the cupboard above and set them on the counter.

"I haven't had ca-fee yet. Is this anything like Coo-coo Coola? Because I did not enjoy that beverage, and I am not interested in stunting my height."

"Stunting..." She had no idea what he meant but wasn't sure she dared ask. "Coffee is nirvana," she said instead, focusing on the subject at hand. "Do you like sweet things, or haven't you discovered your sweet tooth yet?"

He ran a finger down one of his fangs, his frown deepening. "My teeth are not sweet."

"Such a tragedy," she said with a laugh.

Frankly, she was surprised they hadn't felt hard during their kiss. Did he ever use them during play to bite? Something her grannie would disapprove of her asking.

"Why don't I make you a cup the way I like it, and you can see what you think?" she said.

"All right." He tugged out a chair from the table and sat. Yesterday, he was dressed pretty much like an astronaut, in a one-piece flight suit with a hole in the back for his tail. Today, he wore clothing like any Earth guy, jeans custom-made to fit his tall, muscular frame, again with a hole for his tail, plus a t-shirt with *aliens do it better* on the front.

That had to be a joke.

In the literature she was sent, the little bit she'd skimmed, that is, it stated each Cu'zod would be given a complete wardrobe and basic toiletries upon arrival at the spaceport. It was expected the host would provide whatever else they needed after that, deducting as needed from their wages. They were also provided medical care, though there weren't many doctors trained in Cu'zod anatomy. Not yet. But they'd set up a website and a doctor could Skype with someone working at the embassy if need be.

Who had decided to put that saying on his t-shirt, though?

A Night Before Christmas lay on her kitchen table, where she dropped it while they were eating dinner. Likir had opened it and was scrolling through the pages.

She lowered his cup of coffee in front of him, and he stared at the brown liquid.

"Try it. It's yummy."

The flash of his fangs her way made her pulse skip. She focused on holding her coffee cup, worried she was so flustered she'd drop it.

He lifted his cup and sniffed. "It smells pleasant." After taking a sip, he clunked it on the table. The liquid sloshed around. "This… This…"

"Bad or good?" She held her breath, awaiting his answer.

"It is wonderous. Is ca-fee part of Christmas?"

"Coffee is available all year long."

"No," he gasped.

"Sure is. If you want, I'll make you a cup each morning."

He stared at her mouth, and her tongue teased out to lick her lips. Bad Emily, but she couldn't help it with him looking at her like he'd like to devour her.

Pretend. This was pretend!

It sure as hell didn't feel like pretend.

"I would love a cup of this wonder each morning, thank you." He opened the book and pointed to the little guys in brown suits and pointy hats and shoes clustered around Santa. "What are these figures?"

"Elves."

He tilted his head. "What role do these elves play in Christmas magic?"

"In the story of Santa, he lives at the North Pole, which is covered with snow all year round. He spends the year before Christmas creating gifts to give good girls and boys on Christmas eve. The elves live there with him and help him craft the toys."

"They are helpers, then."

"Yes."

"Like me." He flashed his fangs again, and she felt so melty, she worried she'd slid off her chair. "I will help you here with the animals."

"Exactly."

He nodded slowly. "Then in some ways, I am also an elf."

"A big elf."

"Elves are not big like Cu'zods?"

"Nope."

"Hmm."

"If you want, you can wear an elf costume to the Christmas Ball. We're expected to dress up."

His face smoothed. "I would like to do this."

"Then we'll have to go to the mall tomorrow or the next day to buy material to make you a costume." Grannie had been the true seamstress, and Emily had learned from the best.

"Very well. We will embark to this mall and obtain what we need." He studied the elves again, tracing a claw down one of the taller ones. "What will you wear for a cust-oon to the ball?"

"I'm not sure." She wrinkled her nose. "Months ago, before Bradley was kicked to the curb, we talked about the ball. I was going to dress as Mrs. Claus and him Santa." So stupid. Who would've thought Santa was a cheater? "But that's the last way I'd like dress as now."

"Why not be another elf with me?"

It would be easier. She could buy enough material for herself, too. "I like that idea."

"Very well. Then we will be elves together, crafting Christmas goodness for all the boys and girls."

Her laughter burst out, and it was followed by a ding from the stove. She rose and took the muffins out of the oven. Yum, yum, yum.

After plating a few, she placed three in front of Likir and two for herself plus the butter and knives. It didn't take long to peel off the muffin wrapper and slather hers with buttery goodness.

He stared at the muffins, and she swore his mouth watered.

Who wanted a replicator when you could eat things like this?

"Will you mind jingling?" she asked, returning to the elf costume discussion. He was going to be an amazing elf.

"What is this jingle?" he asked as he lifted a piece of muffin.

She loved sharing this season with Likir. Would he be here come spring when her grannie's prized tulips were in bloom? Or during the summer, when she took the dogs to the park and let them run free? Fall was for apple picking and building leaf nests.

He'd be gone by then, moved into his own place and maybe even a better job. She could barely afford to pay herself, though she'd keep him on as long as she could.

And talk about making her feel down. Even a bite of muffin didn't cheer her up.

"Why are you sad?" he asked, his own bite hovering near his mouth.

She pressed for a smile. "I'm not. I mean, you're here, and it's been amazing already. We've got muffins and coffee. Soon, we'll be working with the animals in my rescue. What could be better than that?"

After lowering his muffin back onto his plate, he leaned across the table and glided a band of hair from her face, his claw smooth on her skin. "Yet you are sad. Tell me?"

She couldn't burden him with her troubles. She'd find a way to make this work alone. At least she had enough money for the next few weeks. A month if she was careful. After that, they could talk, or she could call Derrick and tell him she wouldn't be able to continue with the program.

Yeah, that thought gutted her and not only because that meant losing an employee.

She'd miss Likir.

"I…" She could explain a little. "The ball is very important to me and the rescue." No harm in sharing that much. "It costs a lot to run a business like this, and the ball is a chance for me to solicit donations."

"Your rescue is not funded by your government?"

Her bite of muffin almost got stuck, so she washed it down with a gulp of coffee. "I wish they funded it, but no. To keep this place going, I need donations."

"I will help you obtain these donations," he said, which made her smile become true.

"I appreciate it. Just having you here to help is wonderful. Many of the animals are ready for adoption, and prospective families will come by over the next few days to see if they're a good fit. Hopefully, we'll place them in forever homes. You're going to be amazed when you see it happen before your eyes. These animals have lived rough lives. Knowing they'll be loved and cared for makes all the other parts of this job worthwhile."

"This is amazing work. I see this already with Alfred."

He took a bite of his muffin. "This..." One bite and muffin base was gone. Within seconds, the other muffins had been consumed, too.

When he gazed longingly at the remainder on the counter, she got up and brought them over.

They ate in companionable silence, and despite finding no solution to her financing dilemma, her heart felt lighter. Perhaps sharing even a tiny bit helped.

After finishing, Likir carefully lifted Alfred and placed him on his lap. Again, she marveled that the unadoptable dog had taken to a burly Cu'zod warrior.

When he leaned forward to nuzzle the top of Alfred's head, her heart pretty much melted.

It was always hard to say goodbye to an animal she'd grown to love, but she loved showing them some people could be trusted.

Emily had a feeling it was going to rip her heart out to say goodbye to Likir.

Likir

"And that's all you need to do to keep the animals happy," Emily said.

After finishing the muffins, she'd taken him to the animal areas. She'd already been out earlier to put some of the dogs into their runs. A strange term as the dogs merely walked within the areas. He hadn't seen any of them run.

Then she showed him how to feed, water, groom, and provide general care to the animals in her—their—rescue. "I take the dogs for walks at least twice a day, weather permitting, and I have a play area for the cats and kittens. That's a very hands-on thing. The kittens need lots of socialization with humans. If they're super friendly, people are more apt to adopt them."

He'd never seen anything as small as a kee-ten. Yet they were incredibly friendly. One, he named Valicia, after his younger sister. It crawled up his body and perched on his shoulder as he worked. He hadn't had the heart to put her back inside the pen with her siblings. "I will gladly help you do all this."

"I'll be working alongside you." She held one of the

adult cats, a creature with wild eyes who kept making the long sssssss sound at Likir. Puffin, the male was called. His soft, silky hair was black on his back with a white belly. Shifting her hips, she winced.

"You are hurt?" he asked, prepared to blaze through the room to defend her, but there appeared to be no threats.

"I'm okay. I fell yesterday." Her lips thinned. "It was my own fault. I was hurrying."

His chest ached at the thought that she was alone when she was injured, with no one here to soothe her wounds. He'd already seen she gave everything she had to her animal friends, leaving very little behind for herself.

If he could, he'd make sure she felt she had someone near to comfort her when *she* had need.

Puffin snuggled in Emily's arms, something Likir wished he could do. He couldn't help it. The more he was around her, the more he wanted her.

Her fond glance took in the sparkling room. "I've been doing all of this myself for months since my last volunteer moved away. It'll be nice to have a second set of hands to help with the chores." She eased Puffin around and held him out to Likir. "Would you like to hold him?"

He reeled back from the feline. "He makes the ssssss sound." A warning Likir respected after a swipe of Puffin's claws.

"He's just nervous." She nudged her head to a chair on one side of the room. "Have a seat, and I'll put him on your lap. You'll need to get used to each of the animals if you're going to work with them. Puffin puffs up and acts brave, but he's a big baby. He only acts gruff because he was hurt, and he doesn't trust easily."

"Like you?" Likir said, watching her face.

She paused and nodded. "Yeah, like me."

"Brad-lee was foolish to let you go."

"He's a jerk. A cheater. But he's not the only one who betrayed me."

Her parents, he assumed. If they were here, he'd snarl and show them his wrath. How dare they throw away someone so special?

Emily stooped down beside Likir and carefully eased Puffin into his arms. "Pet him like this." While Valicia watched from Likir's shoulder, her tiny motor running in his ear, Emily demonstrated by scratching underneath Puffin's neck. "He loves this and rubs behind his ears."

With utmost care, Likir stroked Puffin. The sssss sound turned into a soft rumble, emitted from the beast's chest.

"What is this rrrrrr sound they all make?" he asked.

Emily's smile was the most beautiful thing he'd ever seen. "It means he likes you."

❄

They took the doo-gees for another walk the next day.

"I am not a good dog walker," Likir said, struggling to untangle himself from a web of leashes. He'd bravely volunteered to take six of the doo-gees while she'd taken the rest.

The kee-ten, Valicia, he'd tucked beneath his coat in a smaller sling. She slept; her tiny body curled against Likir.

One doo-gee was black and his back came to Likir's knees. He lolled his tongue and kept trying to sniff everyone's crotch as they passed on the walkway. This entangled his leash with everyone else because he'd leap from one side of the walk to the other.

Another doo-gee was the size of Likir's foot and continuously yipped, alternating his yips with trying to bite the bigger, black doo-gee's hind legs. Two others...well, Likir couldn't tell them apart. They were bigger than the foot-sized doo-gee but smaller than the black one. The final two walked along sedately, something he was eternally grateful for.

He'd lost track of their names. It was all he could do to keep them from bolting in different directions.

"You're an amazing dog walker," Emily said. Somehow, with almost as many doo-gees on leashes as Likir, and most of them larger than the ones under his control, she kept them in front of her, pacing in a polite manner on the snowy walkway.

The cool air nipped down Likir's spine, and his tail felt frozen already. He enjoyed how cold it was, but his tail was going to need a coat if he walked doo-gees twice daily.

"This is your second full day," Emily said. "No one expects you to be a dog whisperer in less than forty-eight hours."

Alfred, riding in the sling mounted across her chest, poked his head out and seemed to nod in agreement. He loved Emily, and Likir well understood why.

Speaking of the cold...

"Will the weather remain as it is for..." Likir had been about to say forever, but that implied doom. Shivers tracked down his spine despite the winter coat he'd donned, the mee-tins on his hands, and the fuzzy hat Emily had mounted on his head. She'd poked holes in the top for his horns, which was thoughtful, and the pom-chom dangling from the tip of the hat bobbed about his shoulders merrily. When he first wore it, Valicia batted it with her paws.

Emily had snickered when she finished setting it on his head, though he wasn't sure why. He loved how it looked when he examined himself in the mirror.

But the cold... It was too much for a Cu'zod warrior to bear.

"Do you mean all the snow?" she said, stepping over a frozen puddle.

"On Cu'zod, we enjoy a stable temperature. Rarely hot and never this chilled."

"Welcome to Maine." Her smile softened her words. "But to answer your question, no. It'll be chilly here for the next four months or so but then gradually warm up. Lately, it's been blazing hot in the summer, but fall is nice."

"Fall. This is the season prior to this..." hellish, "winter, correct?"

"It is. I can't wait to take you apple picking and pumpkin carving, and you're going to love Halloween..." Her smile faded. "Well, you'll love doing those things wherever you are after leaving my place. I didn't mean you'd be doing them with me."

He wanted to do everything with her, but their pretend relationship didn't allow them to discuss a future together. What was he going to do when she said they were breaking down? No, breaking...*up*. That was the term. He didn't want to break up, either. He wanted to kiss Emily. Sit on the sofa and read more Christmas stories with her.

Take her hand and tug her up to the big bed he slept in alone.

Even walking doo-gees with her was a joy, despite how they pulled his arms in all sorts of directions. He'd take all twelve at once as long as Emily strode by his side.

They passed a couple coming from the other direction, and both their gazes widened. He didn't turn after they passed, but their stares cut into his spine. He was becoming used to being a novelty, but hoped someday, humans would stride past him like they did each other, giving only a brief smile, as if he was someone just like them.

Emily's phoon chimed, and she stopped on the path and answered it. "Oh, hi, Mom." She waved toward Likir. "Do you mind if I take this? You go ahead and finish the loop and pick me up on the way back. She sat on a bench when he nodded, the sedate doo-gees dropping to the ground to rest with her.

He strode forward, trying not to listen, but unable to prevent himself from overhearing.

"No, Mom, I don't want to get back with Bradley. No, Mom, he's not a good guy. I've told you already that…"

Likir cut off the rest with rapid strides, grateful for once that the smallest doo-gee kept yipping.

"Ah, such a lovely day, isn't it?" someone called from his left.

Likir paused and noticed an older male with bushy white hair on his face and head smiling his way. The male walked down his way of the drive, approaching Likir.

"Nippy out but the air invigorates the lungs, doesn't it?" he said. His nod took in the doo-gees winding around Likir's legs. "I'm Stanley."

"I am Likir," he said, dipping his head forward. "It is a pleasure to meet you." That was the greeting he'd practiced while traveling from Cu'zod.

"That's a lot of dogs you have there," Stanley said with a smile. His cheeks were rosy, and his belly round, but Likir had seen other males with a similar appearance on the tee-vee last evening.

"Yes, six," Likir said. "I work at the animal rescue run by Emily Carlisle."

"Ah, Emily. Such a wonderful woman."

"She is amazing," Likir breathed.

"The rescue is a delightful project, a welcome addition to our community."

Likir knew Emily worried about making it a success,

but anyone who saw her work with the animals knew she gave everything her heart. He hoped someday, she'd hand her heart to him.

"Well, I should get back inside," Stanley said. "It was nice meeting you, Likir. I hope we run into each other again."

"Yes, I am sure we will," Likir said, guiding the doo-gees down the sidewalk as Stanley strode up the driveway to his dwelling.

After circumnavigating the neighborhood, he returned to Emily. She sat on the bench, staring forward, the doo-gees sitting placidly around her. Alfred snuggled in his pouch, staring up at her mournfully.

"Are you all right?" Likir said, sitting beside her.

She sniffed and sucked in a breath, releasing it slowly. "Yup. Sometimes…"

"What?" He stroked a band of her silky hair off her face with his claw.

"I should change my number or refuse to talk with her."

"Families can be…complicated."

"They sure can." Standing, she forced a smile onto her face. "Let's get back, shall we? I think your tail is cold."

"All of me is cold," he said, pushing to sound cheerful. He hated seeing her sad, hated that her mother could make her feel this way instead of joyful.

Their pace slow, they returned to her dwelling with the doo-gees.

A blue car waited in the driveway. As they approached, a woman climbed out. She smiled nervously as they approached, her gaze scanning the doo-gees as if seeking…something. Likir wasn't sure what.

"I'm sorry I'm early, but I couldn't wait," she said. Her attention fell on him. "Oh, my. I've…" Her pink cheeks went darker. "I'm sorry. You must be one of the Cu'zods. I... It's lovely to meet you."

He dipped his head forward, still trying to keep the doo-gees from entangling their leashes and choking each other. At least the smallest one had stopped yipping. "I am Likir. It is very lovely to meet you, as well."

"I'm Mandy." She lifted her chin toward Emily. "I called last week about meeting the dogs available for adoption?"

"It's nice to meet you," Emily said.

"I'm sorry I'm early." Her gaze shot to the back of her car. "We couldn't wait."

"It's no problem," Emily said. "After Likir and I put the others in their runs, we'll bring out the male who's available for adoption. Do you want to wait inside?"

"Oh, I'll wait out here if that's okay."

"Sure," Emily said. "You said you have a child about ten-years-old?" Her gaze scanned the car, and Likir sensed movement in the back seat.

The door opened, and little legs projected out, followed by a female stripling. He'd seen pictures of Earthling striplings but had yet to meet one. They hadn't seen any during their walks.

She took a few steps toward them as they walked up the drive but said nothing, just stared, her small mouth opening to a circle.

"Let's wait in the car, Sarah," Mandy said. Rounding the vehicle, she took the stripling's hand and helped her back inside, the stripling peering at him and Emily.

"Cross your fingers they fall in love," Emily whispered as the car doors shut.

He wasn't completely sure what she meant, but she'd mentioned someone was coming to the dwelling today to meet one of the doo-gees. Others would arrive over the next few days to meet cats, kee-tens, and other doo-gees. Emily so wanted to place some of her animal friends in loving homes for the holidays.

He still wasn't completely sure he understood the meaning of this wonderous event she called Christmas, but he was eager to find out.

They took the doo-gees to the back entrance where Emily quickly unclipped them one-by-one and either put them in their runs or into a crate, depending on the temperament of the creature—something she'd explained earlier, and he was still trying to solidify in his mind. Only the black doo-gee remained on a leash.

On Cu'zod, every creature roamed free, and none were penned. But Likir could tell by their wide eyes and cautious stances that these poor animals had lived tough lives. Shadows haunted their eyes, and when they looked at him, seeking his attention, his heart broke.

Loving containment could actually provide comfort, Emily told him earlier, and from what he'd seen, they thrived.

"I'll come back after they leave, and we can finish up the grooming," Emily said. "Let's take this dog inside. I want to show you some Christmas magic—assuming things go as they should." She led the black doo-gee inside, the creature bouncing by her hip. In the kitchen, she handed Likir the leash and kept her voice low. "Don't let him jump on Mandy or Sarah if you can help it."

He wasn't sure he could prevent such an occurrence. This creature appeared to have springs at the base of his legs, instead of paws.

"I'll let them inside," she added.

After removing her coat and hanging it up, she smoothed her hair and unlocked and opened the front door. She waved, and the bang of car doors rang out.

"Welcome," she said as they approached. "Come on in."

Likir carefully shucked his coat, keeping a hold on the leash, and draped his coat on the back of a chair. The doo-gee watched him intently, his tail flicking back and forth on the floor. He advanced into the opening between the living room and kitchen, watching as Mandy settled on the sofa, keeping the stripling tight to her side.

"Would you like to meet the dog, Sarah?" Mandy asked in a cajoling voice as her arm encircled the small child.

Sarah shrugged her mother away. She rose and drifted to the window to stare outside.

"The Christmas music is a nice touch, by the way." Mandy's voice dropped off to a hush. "Sarah is…we've had a tough time since her dad…died." Tears welled in her eyes and every bit of love she felt for her daughter shone on her face. "I'm hoping a pet will help her heal. Me, too, frankly. Nothing will replace Dave, of course, but we have room in our hearts to love another. That's why I chose your rescue, Emily. You're helping creatures who've had a tough life find hope for a better future. I'm hoping you can do the same with us."

"This time of year can be magical, all on its own," Emily said, joining him in the opening to the living quarters. She stooped down and rubbed the black doo-gee's ears. The creature sighed and leaned into her touch. "There's something special about a pet, don't you think? Dogs give everything they have inside them. They love deeply, and sometimes, I think they're capable of performing their own kind of magic."

Mandy nodded, and her attention went to Likir and then the black doo-gee whose soft brown gaze traveled between Mandy and Sarah.

"This is the fella I was talking about," Emily said. She kissed the doo-gee's snout. "He was found wandering the city with an injured paw. He snapped at everyone when he was taken to the local vet. They called me because he wouldn't let anyone approach him." She stroked the doo-gee's face and neck, and the creatures huffed softly with pleasure.

Likir didn't feel even one twinge of jealousy. It was clear Emily's heart overflowed with affection for each of the creatures in her care. Who would deny them this right to pure love?

"I've worked hard with him over the past six months and look at him now." Emily kissed his snout, then buried her face in the doo-gee's neck, speaking so low, only Likir could hear. "I'm gonna miss you, baby, if they take you to your forever home, but I'll be so freakin' happy for you. You need this, maybe as much as they need you."

She straightened and swiped at her eyes, smiling through her tears. "I call him Josh, but of course you can name him whatever you want. If you choose to take him home, I suggest you start by calling him Josh-Sammy, or whatever name you choose. Over time, you could drop Josh and he'll come to Sammy."

Sarah turned from the window. Her panicked gaze fell on her mom before smoothing, then drifted to Likir and the doo-gee. She swallowed deeply, and the longing on her face couldn't be hidden.

Though this wasn't necessarily part of their plan, Likir stepped forward with Josh beside him, approaching the timid stripling. He stopped a few paces away.

"Would you like to touch Josh?" he asked softly, taking care not to make sudden movements that would startle the child. "He loves to be petted."

Alfred poked his head from Emily's doo-gee sling and

watched them, not barking or snapping or snarling, his usual demeanor with anyone other than Emily and now, Likir.

If she hoped to place Alfred in a forever home, it would be some time before he was ready.

Sarah stepped toward Josh; her hand outstretched.

Mandy clutched her hands to her throat, tears shimmering in her eyes. She said nothing, just left this to her daughter.

"Josh is a nice name," Sarah said softly.

Mandy gasped, and Likir wondered how long it had been since Sarah spoke. Perhaps since the loss of Dave?

Josh whined softly and shifted forward on the floor, not standing but moving himself with his front feet while remaining sitting. He didn't stop until he was within touching distance of Sarah. He waited patiently, perhaps to give the stripling the time she needed.

As Emily said, he must've suffered considerable abuse before he found his way to her rescue. She said he hadn't stopped snapping at her for nearly a month.

Who would do horrible things to a defenseless creature?

Sarah dropped to her knees and held out both hands to Josh. "Come, doggie?" She dashed a look up at Likir as if seeking approval.

He held himself still, letting her choose the pace of this interaction. While he'd never worked at a rescue, he did know creatures, having tamed many in the forest while on land or in the waters surrounding his family's estates.

Sarah carefully stroked Josh's head and ears. She turned a delighted smile Likir's way. "Soft."

"He is," Likir said. Because he felt like he towered over the stripling, he dropped down to sit on the floor. This put him at the level of this half-grown Earthling. "His belly is soft, too."

Josh must truly be magical because he seemed to understand Likir's words. He laid down and rolled onto his back, presenting his belly, a position that must show trust as a doo-gee's belly was soft and vulnerable to attack. One swipe of a Cu'zod's claws could rip the defenseless creature wide open.

Sarah scooted forward and rubbed Josh's belly while the doo-gee wiggled with pleasure.

"Look at that," Mandy said. "I hoped but…" Her hand reached out, and Emily finished the bridge stretching between them, two females sharing this amazing moment. "What do you think, Sarah?" Mandy's voice trembled. "Do you think Josh should join us for Christmas?"

Sarah nodded, never taking her attention off Josh. "What a good doggie."

"What do you need from me?" Mandy asked, releasing Emily's hand.

"I have a few papers you'll need to fill out, but we can do that in the kitchen." Emily stood, and her gaze met his. He could tell she sought approval to leave him here with Josh and Sarah, and he nodded.

Mandy rose and followed Emily into the kitchen. Their murmured voices drifted into the living room, but they didn't eclipse the Christmas music emitted from the tee-vee. Likir was coming to love this music.

They returned not long after. Mandy held a plastic bag with what Emily told him earlier contained a starter kit for adopted pets, including food, a leash, and a few doo-gee toys. The kits were created from donations to the rescue.

Everything here was maintained with donations, and Likir had to wonder how Emily was able to keep it going if her government didn't contribute financial support.

"It's time to go, Sarah," Mandy said.

Sarah dropped down to lay with Josh, her arms encircling his torso. "I don't want to leave him, Mom."

"You don't have to, honey. He's going home with us."

Bouncing up to a sitting position, Sarah's wide-eyed gaze traveled from her mother to Josh. "He is?"

"Yes, honey. He's going to be our dog, now."

"Do we have to bring him back after Christmas?" Sarah's fingers tangled in the fur at Josh's neck.

"Nope. He's staying with us forever." She leaned against Emily's shoulder. "Thank you. I'd like to send a small donation, if that's okay, so you can continue doing this wonderful work for other families."

"Of course," Emily said. "Anything is welcome."

Mandy nodded pertly. "I'll send something out first thing tomorrow." She crossed the room and clipped Josh's leash to his harness. "Ready, Sarah? It's time to get this good boy home, where he belongs."

Sarah rose to her feet and held out her hand for the leash.

As Likir and Emily stood in the open doorway and watched the three walk down the path, he marveled at how well-behaved Josh was.

The good doo-gee didn't strain even once on his leash.

"I'm going to miss him," Emily sniffed.

Likir put his arm around her shoulders and gave her a quick hug.

"I know there are three more dogs outside somewhere who could take his place, but he's special."

As Mandy's vehicle backed down the driveway, Likir turned Emily to face him.

He kissed her forehead then held her tight as she cried.

9

Emily

"Why don't we go into the living room and put up the tree?" Emily asked Likir after a dinner of veggie burgers and fries. She'd wanted to do it the night before, but time slipped away. Tired after her fall in the kennel and the confrontation with Bradley, she'd put it off until today.

But now it was time to stop moping about Josh. He'd found a forever home, and she couldn't ask for anything better than that. Each animal she took in stole a piece of her heart. Only bringing in another in desperate need restored it. It wasn't a cycle or a duty to Emily. She loved seeing a creature find trust in those around them. No, find love.

Would she ever find love herself? She wasn't completely broken like those in her care, but she still wanted to find her heart a forever home.

She couldn't stop thinking about Likir finding a forever home with her.

It was useless to let her mind wander in this direction. Dangerous. And it would rip a piece out of her she'd never replace when he left. She needed to stop this train of thought immediately, before it was too late.

She was determined to show Likir the meaning of Christmas, and it sure wasn't about mourning. She'd shed her tears for Josh. It was time to celebrate that he'd found a new family who'd love him always.

"I'm sorry. You want to put up what where?" Likir asked.

Beneath the table, Alfred stirred in his bed. He'd fallen asleep after sniffing at his kibble then chowing down on the minced-up chicken Likir insisted on feeding him. His soft snores drifted around them.

"By the way," he said. "I love these frees dipped in this red sauce." He swiped a curly fry she'd cooked in the oven through the hillside of ketchup on his plate.

As if she couldn't tell. "I have plenty of the red sauce. I'll make sure to add it to my table from now on."

"I appreciate that." He sounded serious, but humor sparkled in his eyes.

"Wait until you try spaghetti sauce and salsa." So many culinary wonders she looked forward to sharing with him.

She couldn't get over the quantity of food he ate. It reminded her of her grannie sharing stories about Emily's grandfather packing away a family-sized dish of chicken casserole that was intended for four. She'd had to reheat leftovers to make up a meal for the others.

"You are sure this has no ham in this?" he asked for what had to be the twentieth time. "I am not eating a pig?"

"I told you I don't eat meat." While she'd grown up consuming everything from bacon to steak, she couldn't stomach eating a creature now that she cared for so many.

"I do not understand the name, then. Hamburgler."

"Veggie *burger*. I said burger originally and mentioned that most people eat hamburgers."

"Yes, yes. Burgler."

"This is made of ground up beans and...I'm not sure what else," she said, wishing now she'd read the back of the package. "Spices."

"Which spices?" He examined the bit left of his third "burgler," and she held in her laugh. For someone skeptical about them, he'd sure eaten his fair share—dipped in ketchup, of course. He'd also put ketchup on his mac 'n cheese last night, which she smiled about because her grannie had done that, too.

"Which spices?" she said. "I'd say garlic powder, onion powder, and some kind of Cajun mix as they're spicy."

"I like the zippy component." He tapped his finger on his tongue. "I presume that is the fire I feel here?"

His tongue was long and thick.

She shouldn't be thinking of all the things he could do with it. Naughty Emily was going to get coal in her stocking for sure.

Or maybe she'd get Likir in her stocking? She'd enjoy pulling him out on Christmas morning.

Sadly, Santa was not going to visit her home this year or any other. Kids believed in him. Emily did not.

Enough. There she went again, letting her sadness about Josh bring her down. She'd miss him, but Mandy said she'd bring him by to visit in a month or so, after he was settled. Emily could smooch him and tell him she loved him again.

Rising, she took their plates to the sink. She turned to face Likir, leaning back against the counter. "As for the tree, it's fake, like I said, but it's pretty. No needles dropping on the floor, which is a bonus."

He frowned. "I have been watching these Christmas stories on the tee-vee."

"When?" They'd been busy over the past few days,

grooming the dogs, playing with the cats, interacting with the kittens, and cleaning out pens and runs, in addition to taking the dogs for walks. She'd barely had time to breathe.

"During my break times."

Which she'd insisted on. He kept saying he wanted to continue helping, but everyone needed to step away from their job every now and then. Besides, it was the law.

"How many Christmas shows were you able to watch during four fifteen-minute breaks? They were short."

"I saw small portions of seven. In them, I could see that to have a full Christmas, one must have a real tree, not a fake."

Well, it went with them fake dating, right? And fake kissing.

Wait. The kiss hadn't felt fake. She wanted to do it again. Perhaps she should suggest they needed more practice.

"Christmas is in your heart, not in the physical things around you," she said. Something she needed to remember herself. "Like the feelings I get when I think of my grannie. Yes, I miss her, but I got to spend the last few years making her life special. No one can take that away."

The only thing that might be taken away from Emily was this building if she didn't find funding. It would hurt to sell the house, to pack up the things she'd come to love while living here with her grandmother.

"I see I am distressing you with talk of a true tree," he said, rising. "I don't wish to do that." He walked over to stand in front of her. He smelled good, despite mucking out pens and handling dogs all day. It was him, this heady scent. Pure Likir.

"It's not that." Was there any harm in sharing some of her burden? Sometimes, she worried it would drag her down to the ground and never release her. "Let's go upstairs and carry down the ornaments and the boxed tree. We can set it up then decide if it stays or if we need to get something else. While we do it, I want to tell you a bit about what I'm going through."

He braced his palms on the counter on either side of her hips. "I do not like seeing you sad."

There was nothing to be done about it. Talking to him about her troubles would lessen her fears, but nothing could take them away.

Their gazes met, and for this one moment, she wished with all her heart that this was real, that he was her boyfriend, that he cared only for her, that what they had would grow into something incredibly special. The warm feeling encompassed her like his body did now.

"Emily…" His head dropped lower, and he paused, his soft breath teasing her face. "I want to kiss you for real, if I may."

"Likir…" She groaned and pressed herself against him.

That was all the invitation he needed. His mouth came down on hers, softer than she expected. His lips felt amazing; smooth and warm. When his tongue dipped out to touch, she opened her lips and let him in.

Excitement boiled inside her, and she feared she'd burst.

They stumbled into the living room, their mouths still connected, their hands feverish on each other's bodies.

Tumbling down onto the sofa, she ended up straddling him with her thighs on either side of his hips.

She should pull away. Remind him they had a boss and employee relationship. But all she could think about was ripping off his clothing and exploring his scales.

They kissed, deep strokes of their tongues shouting out their desire.

She moaned and pressed her groin against his, savoring the feel of the steel inside his pants. From this simple touch, she could tell it was big, pulsing. She wanted him buried deep inside her.

His tail coiled up and tucked between her legs. The forked tip stroked across her clit, a hard, quivering thing. Only her clothing separated them.

She keened in his mouth, and he captured the sound and pulled it inside him.

His hands glided up her sides and inward, toward her breasts. He cupped them through her shirt and bra, his firm claws stroking her nipples.

She pumped against his tail; overcome with a wildness she couldn't deny. Ripping her mouth away from his, she straightened and rode him, pulsing her hips against his tail while the tip rubbed against her clit.

His fingers... His claws... Her nipples tightened. Everything inside her spiraled toward a feeling that would never be denied.

She came, a body wracking, quivering explosion that shook her to her core.

A wanton, feral sound was jerked from her throat, and she savored it as she crashed through to the other side.

10

Likir

*C*olor rode high in Emily's cheeks, and her body still quivered.

When she collapsed on his chest, he held her, stroking her back while his tail teased along her spine.

Some would say this never should've happened.

They couldn't seem to help themselves. If anything, he shouldn't have strode over to the counter and kissed her. But her forlorn tone and the bleakness on her face had tugged at something deep inside him. All he could think of was giving her comfort.

He'd done that now, in a primal way, at least. Someday, he hoped to do it with the strength of his arms and the shelter of his heart.

"I'm sorry," she said, her voice husky.

"I hope you do not regret what happened." He had to name it. Speak of it. He couldn't allow any dismay on her part to fester.

"All right, so, this might sound strange, but I'm not sorry we just did *this*." Her hand flicked between them. "What I'm sorry about is that you're still hard while I'm savoring fulfillment." Her eyes darkened. "Could I do the same for you?"

He sat up, keeping her in his arms. She faced him with her legs still wrapped around him. Yes, he ached, but he didn't wish to push this. They hadn't known each other long, though he already knew he could care deeply for her.

"I am fine," he said, a nice, neutral response. He didn't dare say much else. All he could think of was how close her warm wetness was to his cock. All that mattered was that she'd found pleasure with him, something that made him feel like roaring out his joy.

"This doesn't feel fine." She nudged herself against him, and her breath caught. "You're inflamed. It must be uncomfortable." Easing back on his lap, her hands went to the waistband of his pants. "May I…"

All he could do was jerk out a nod. His cock was figuratively killing him. He ached to bury it deeply inside her, to ride her like she just did him, until he joined her in bliss.

Don't push it, right?

He was doomed. Pushing and pulling and riding her was all he could dream of.

Her fingers kept gliding along the finer scales on his abs. They were warm and he wanted them all over his body.

"May you…?" he asked, his mind a blur.

"I want to touch you," she said. When she looked up at him, she bit down on her lower lip. It was his undoing.

"Yes." He kissed her again, drinking in her heat and passion, trying to imprint it on his mind forever.

She leaned back and looked down. Her hands fumbled with the fastener at the top of his pants before she got it open. It didn't help that his engorged cock strained against the fabric.

A zipppp sound, and he sprang free of the constraints binding him.

"Oh," she said.

For a moment, he worried he wasn't enough for her. He'd heard of this happening.

"I'm too small," he said.

She giggled; a free, easy sound that made his worry disappear like early morning mist on the Tigest River. "Size doesn't matter, but there's no way anyone would complain about this beauty."

His face twisted. "You are beautiful. I am not sure any cock holds true beauty."

She scooted back and dropped her feet to the floor, bending down between his spread legs. "Let me show you what I see." Her finger glided along his length. "It's blue and lightly scaled."

"All of me is blue and has varying scaling. More on my chest, back, and head, for protection, but I am this way all over."

"How about the bottom of your feet?"

He frowned, never having considered that. "Not there."

"You're distracting me from your amazing cock." Her grin flickered across her face. "Let me get closer to examine it fully." Her breath coasted across the tip, and his hips jerked up. "This rounded bit on the end is intriguing." She peeked up at him before returning to her examination. "I can almost feel it inside me, stretching me."

He groaned. This teasing talk made him want to strip her, lick her entire body, then plunder himself deep inside her. *Then* she would feel the stretch.

"What's this?" she asked, her fingers smoothing down his length. She rubbed at the base.

"A blinder nub."

She rolled it between her fingers, and it responded, vibrating and twitching. "Whoa. It's thick, like a big thumb, and about an inch and a half in length. What does it do?" Only wonder filled her voice. He liked that his body intrigued her.

"It will attach to your clit and remain there, vibrating."

"I..." She shook her head and wonder filled her face. "Honestly, I'd like to try this out someday soon."

He'd offer now, but again, he did not wish to rush this. She was like the finest merdeen, a rich beverage to be sipped and savored as it coasted down his throat, before lifting the glass again for another taste.

His cock had other ideas. It bobbed up, seeking whatever warmth it could find.

Her hands wrapped around him, and he groaned. When she pumped her fingers from the base to the tip, his brain shot through the top of his head. He couldn't take it. Like a stripling, he'd spend himself in seconds.

"This blinder nub," she said with a frown. "Does it enjoy touch as well?"

"I suppose so."

One side of her mouth quirked up. "Are you telling me you haven't touched it to find out?"

He groaned, a mix of desire and agreement. "It does enjoy touch."

She leaned forward. "How about a tongue?" Her fine, blunted white teeth nibbled on the end, and he thought he'd shoot his seed across the room right then. "Oh, it *is* responsive," she declared, the hum of her mouth transmitting itself through him.

While her hand milked his cock, she sucked the blinder nub fully inside her warm wetness. It sought within her, like it would with her clit, elongating to glide across the soft tissue on the inside of her mouth.

Pulling away, she grinned up at him. "This is amazing. You're amazing."

"I am a simple Cu'zod male."

"Honey, there's nothing simple about you." Easing back, she centered her mouth over his cock. No one had ever...

He shook his head, and his tail looped around her thigh, the tip climbing higher. Would she think him too bold if he undid her pants and sought her body beneath the fabric?

As she sucked the end of his cock deep inside her mouth, it seemed silly to hold anything back.

It would be a challenge to do this with his eyes rolling back in his head, however. Her incredible mouth... Her tongue... She savored and licked and nibbled as she pumped her head over him. He couldn't take much more. He had to be buried inside her.

Not yet, some vaguely rational part of his mind reminded him.

She released him, her mouth emitting a wet, sucking sound. "Come for me like I just did for you." Command came through in her voice, but she didn't need to ask. He'd spill himself within her however she offered.

He would bring her along with him, however. He needed to feel her falling apart.

He leaned forward and loosened her pants.

While her mouth moved on his cock, she wiggled against his hands, helping her pants drop down to her knees. Like she knew exactly what he planned, she kicked the pants to the side and spread her legs wide.

It was all he could do to think, to breathe. He was going to fall apart before he brought her with him.

No, he wouldn't do that.

Think of war or deadly creatures, he commanded himself. *Of treaties and important documents that need to be signed.*

It didn't help. Her mouth worked him like the finest instrument, and he was about to shout out the tune.

The tip of his tail tweaked her clit, and she moaned, her mouth sending shockwaves through him.

He was so close. Incredibly close. He couldn't hold himself back. Leaning his spine against the cushions, he pumped up to meet her mouth, giving his tail free rein. Her hair fanned around her face, brushing against his thighs, creating sensual pleasure.

His tail slipped between her wet folds, seeking deep within her.

She ground down on him while her tongue and mouth went faster.

He pumped within her mouth while driving himself up into her. With each stroke, he flicked his tail across her slit then dipped it inside her.

She gyrated against him, an untamed creature in need of what only he could deliver. It was all he could do not to lift her up and plunge her body down on his cock.

Impale her.

Her aroused scent drove him on. Until she came again, he wouldn't let go himself.

She moved faster, her moans feverish, her body gipping and releasing his tail while her mouth brought him to the very edge of his world and hers combined.

With a shudder, she came again, quivering and shaking around his tail.

He gave in himself, shooting his seed into her mouth.

11

Emily

Should she be embarrassed that she just sucked Likir off while riding his tail? Maybe.

Or maybe not.

She didn't feel embarrassed. She wanted to do it again.

Her need for him was building to an insurmountable level. She couldn't find a way to fight or deny it, and frankly, she was no longer sure she wanted to.

Yet… It was going to hurt to tell him goodbye. Nothing this good ever lasted. Her parents never cared. She'd lost her grannie. Bradley had never been hers. He'd cheated his way across town while letting her think she mattered.

"Don't do this to yourself," she whispered.

"Tell me," he said softly. "I want to know everything."

After tugging up her pants, she'd climbed into his lap and wrapped her legs around him. His cock continued to twitch, and it was all she could do not to strip and climb onto him. Sink down over him this time.

She rested in his arms, her hands on his shoulders, her head against his chest where his heart beat in a furious rhythm.

"What would you like to know?" she asked.

"Why your sadness and joy jumble together so often."

"That's a big ask."

"Too big?"

Not after what they just did together. Sex didn't always equate with intimacy, but with her and Likir, she felt closer to him than before.

It made her feel vulnerable, and she wasn't sure she liked that feeling.

Please take chances in life, her grannie said as she neared death. *Don't hold yourself back, honey, because before you know it, it'll be too late.*

Grannie had loved someone after Emily's grandfather was killed while serving in the military. Whoever it was, it hadn't worked out, and Grannie never said why. But she kept a worn picture of a man in her bedside table. With tattered edges, it was faded, as if someone had repeatedly run their fingers across his face.

Had she lost him, too? Emily would never know.

Easing off Likir's lap, Emily sat beside him. She wanted to see his face as she shared, but frankly, she needed a bit of distance. Sitting in his lap almost fused her to him, the lines between her and him blurring.

He fastened his pants then took her hand.

How much did she dare tell him? Her instincts suggested everything, but she couldn't bare herself to anyone that much. Might as well jump off the cliff and into the deep end of the lake, though, with some of what was bothering her.

"As I've said, I support my rescue with donations," she said. That was nice and neutral. From what she'd shared already, he must suspect donors were her sole source of funding. "I've lived with my grandmother for most of my life. After I'd graduated from high school, I worked at a coffee shop in town. Grannie only had social security, and I wanted to help, so I gave her most of my wages. I didn't realize she saved them all. After I'd volunteered for six years at a nearby rescue, she offered me money, suggesting it was time for me to fulfill my dream and create the animal and grooming areas you see today."

She peered up at him. "I thought she was giving me her life savings, but it was the money I'd paid her for all those years. I discovered this after she died. But when she offered it, no, insisted I take it, I jumped off the cliff, so to speak, using it and grants to get started."

"What is a grant?"

Alfred strolled into the room from the kitchen, yawning. He sat in front of her, and the look on his face said, *Where have you been? Why did I wake up in the kitchen by myself? And…Can I have more chicken?*

She scooped him up, and he circled three times on her lap before settling. "A grant is a way of applying for money that's essentially a gift. You don't have to pay it back. I wrote letters, explaining why they should help support my cause. If they agree, they give me the money. Grants can be written for all sorts of things, but I specified starting my rescue and supporting it on an ongoing basis."

"You said your government doesn't provide this help. Your community doesn't either?" He appeared puzzled.

"Somewhat. There are funds available locally, but they're very limited and not enough to buy more than a bit of food for the animals. They can't offer anywhere near the amount I need to keep the rescue going. It's costly. There are many vet bills, oil to heat the house, utilities, and the cleaning service." The last was her one splurge, though they only came a few times a week.

"So strange," he said. "On Cu'zod, support for something like this would be given without asking."

Imagine living in a community like that. No, imagine not worrying about how she'd support her business beyond the next few weeks. Sometimes, she lay awake well into the night, stressing about how she'd pay the electric or vet bills.

"Here on Earth, we have to solicit funding unless we can provide it ourselves."

"Ah," he said with a nod. "You are fortunate your grandmother supported you in this."

"I started volunteering when I was a teenager at animal shelters, where I learned about rescue operations. The more I discovered, the more I knew I wanted to do my part to help injured creatures find the loving homes they deserve. Grannie was one hundred percent in support of this. She loved the kittens and would sneak them into her room at night to sleep with her. Like you and Valicia."

"You noticed."

"You can keep her in your bed at night if you want."

He chuckled. "I may do that." His face sobered. "Your grandmother sounds like she was a wonderful person."

Emily flashed him a smile. "She was. I miss her so much. She was sharp as a tack until the day she died. While some of the elderly get dementia or Alzheimer's, making them forget much of their lives, my grandmother never did. Her body failed her instead." Emily sighed. "I guess it's not a true failure. She lived to be ninety-three, and that's old for humans. She was in a lot of pain before she died, and that was sad to watch." Her mind dragged her back to setting her alarm at night so she could bring Grannie her medicine that kept her slightly more comfortable and allowed her to remain mobile. Of taking her to PT and doing all she could to make her grandmother's last days easier.

"I'm sorry," he said, taking her hand and squeezing it. "It is a blessing to be loved that much."

It truly was. Emily had never doubted her grandmother's affection.

"When she died, she gave me this house and what she had left in the bank. That and grants carried my business for two years, which is amazing. I've homed over fifty animals in that time, giving them the lives they deserve."

"I can already see the joy you give others," he said. "Mandy and Sarah's hearts will heal with Josh in their lives, and I bet others waiting in the animal areas will soon find homes where they can continue to heal."

"I hope so. I know my animal buddies don't know it's Christmas. That day is like any other to them. But I know. My heart breaks just a little to think of them waiting in cages or runs when they could be racing around a Christmas tree or playing in the snow with kids. They need open pastures to run though, a sofa to sit on and snuggle with someone giving them endless pats, and a warm bed at night to sleep in."

"You do most of this already."

"I can't bring them all into my house, as much as I'd like to. There are too many of them. This is the best situation. They need their own space, a place where they feel safe and secure, then plenty of love to help overcome their past in between."

"You need this, too."

She shrugged and flashed him a smile. "Maybe." Sucking in a breath, she released it fast. "Grannie's money ran out a year ago, but by then, I'd met Bradley. He's wealthy, but that never mattered to me. He supported the rescue over the past year, but he's cut off the funding."

"You worry you will lose everything."

"Yeah." Tears smarted in her eyes. "I've written a ton of grants, and I've been awarded some, but times have been tough for a lot of people lately. What I have coming in isn't enough to support the rescue. I don't take a salary." Defensiveness came through in her voice. "I scrimp as much as I can, but there's never enough."

He frowned. "There must be a way." Lifting her hand, he kissed her knuckles. "We will find it together."

12

Likir

*A*fter talking, Emily suggested they wait until the next day to bring down the tree. They went to their separate beds, Likir with the kee-ten and Emily with Alfred. While he wanted to invite her to share the bigger bed with him, sadness still haunted her. And despite their new intimacy, their relationship was still very new.

The next day was spent as the ones prior, working with the animals. More families came and all the kee-tens other than his favorite were adopted, plus three adult cats, something Emily told him was unusual as many preferred kee-tens. This left them with six cats and one kee-ten still hoping for forever homes.

Two more dogs were adopted, bringing their number to nine, including Alfred.

Sadly, Emily said it was common to see an increase in animals dropped off in the first few months after the holidays. Families would get a pet as a holiday gift then decide it wasn't working out. She expected they'd be busy over the next few months.

The next evening, after an interesting meal of chil-ee,

which he adored, topped with cream of the sour, they sat in the living room again with Alfred and Valicia between them, the two beasties curled together. Soon, he and Emily would bring down the tree, and Likir was interested in watching this decking process.

When Likir abdicated his role in the royal family, he gave up everything that came with being royal, most specifically the wealth his family had enjoyed for many generations. They shared a considerable amount with their people, but the core of their riches remained for them to use as they chose.

Earth was a fresh start. Likir wanted to be like any other Cu'zod settling here.

He also wanted to help Emily. Revealing himself as a prince could help bring in donations, but did he want to do this?

"I will not take a salary from the rescue, either." He hoped this would please her.

"No way," she said, rising. She stood and faced him, her hands on her hips. "You need to be paid and besides, it's required for participation in the settlement program. Without a salary, you can't purchase what you need or find your own apartment."

"Nothing says I cannot remain here with you, correct?" Perhaps he pushed too much by making this statement, but he didn't want to move out in a few months' time. He wanted to stay with Emily if she wanted him here with her, as an employee, just a friend, or her lover. No, he wanted her as his forever mate. What they had was new, however. They'd barely scratched the surface of each other.

How long did it take to fall in love with someone? Already, he knew he could love Emily. Did she feel the same? He wanted to ask but would wait. They had plenty of time.

"You're a special guy, Likir," she said with a soft smile. She stretched her hand to him, and he took it, bridging the small gap between them. "I want you here for as long as you wish to remain."

Neutral, but he'd take it.

"But I have to pay you a regular wage. Thank you for offering, though."

He grumbled, but he wouldn't ask her to break the rules.

"Let's bring down the tree and ornaments," she said. "Then we can go to the mall for material to make elf costumes."

"All right." He rose, and they went to her a-teek, a cool, darker room above the bedrooms, accessed by a tiny set of stairs.

"Cu'zod dwellings are nothing like these houses Earthlings live in," he said as he took a box from her marked orn-ee-ments.

She placed a taller box near the top of the stairs. "What do your houses look like?"

"Many of us live beneath the water, as you know."

"I read that, and I think it's amazing." She paused and stared his way. Sunlight streamed through the solitary window, igniting bits of dust in the air, and haloing her.

His heart ached as he looked at her. In the short time he'd known her, she'd come to mean so much to him.

"You don't have gills, though," she said.

"Some Cu'zods do. Tentacles, too."

"Huh," she said, her gaze traveling his length. He had to bend over to avoid hitting his head on the ceiling, though his horns brushed the rough boards as he moved. "You don't have tentacles either."

He flashed his fangs. "You are correct."

"I read you worked on a farm. That's why you were a

good candidate for my rescue, but I haven't been able to figure out how you farm underwater. I assume crops and creatures?"

"Yes. There are forests beneath the sea. Much of Cu'zod is underwater, though some choose to live on the small bits of land. Since many of us do not have gills, we use a specific plant to provide oxygen when we leave our underwater cities."

"You're a bit like mermaids but also not." She started down the stairs, carrying a box, and he followed with two boxes of his own. "Does your tail help you swim?"

"That, and the webbing between the toes of many Cu'zods."

"I need to see this."

He chuckled as they reached the second story landing. "I will be happy to share my toes with you." Everything, actually. In return, he wanted to explore every bit of Emily's body.

"Tell me about your underwater cities. What do they look like?"

"Our homes and cities are in air-filled spaces deep beneath the waves, what you call domes. Those without gills are able to walk about, breathing easily. Vegetation provides the air we need."

"This sounds incredible," she exclaimed, lowering the box onto the sofa. He did the same with the ones he carried. "I'd love to see one of your underwater cities someday."

"I believe travel will eventually be permitted between our planets, more than just selective settlement for a few."

"I'd be on the first ship," she said, grinning. "Would you..." She sucked in a breath then released it with her words. "If I can someday travel to Cu'zod, will you go with me and show me some of your world?"

He dipped forward in a short bow. "It would be an honor. You asked about our houses. While some choose to live in constructed dwellings within the domes, others live across the floor of the sea in living pods that can be moved based on our wishes. We can take them to the surface or move them about, depending on what view we want to see outside our version of windows. If you love the forest, you move your pod there. Do you wish to view and perhaps work with coral reefs and fish of ever color imaginable? Move to that location. Others choose to settle their pods near the fields they till on the islands. My family has clusters of pods in vast underwater valleys, as well as some in the mountain ranges beneath the sea. Still others are located on many of the bits of land dotting our seas."

He chose not to use the word "estate" because he didn't wish to brag about his family's wealth that was no longer his. By giving up his status with the royal family, it meant he could not offer Emily everything she needed to sustain the rescue forever.

There must be a way he could help, but he couldn't think of what it could be.

"Cu'zod sounds like a beautiful place," she said.

He would love to share it with her. Share everything with her, and one day, perhaps, he would. While he had abdicated his role in the royal family, they still loved him and he them. He was welcome at their estates, and his grandmother had insisted he not give up everything. He still had a small home in the Briar Reef, where he could stay whenever he visited Cu'zod.

It was too easy to picture him lying in his vast bed with Emily nestled in his arms, staring through the clear roof at the world around them. The beauty of the undersea cities of Cu'zod could not be easily described. One had to live there to fully understand.

"I will retrieve the final box from the a-teek?" he asked.

"Thanks." Her warm gaze traveled down his body, and he wanted to tug her back to the sofa and spread her wide so he could taste her. Take her to the king bed and love her all night long.

Perhaps someday.

Returning to the living quarters with the box, he lowered it to the floor beside the sofa.

"What do we do now?" he asked.

"Set up the tree and decorate it." She turned on the tee-vee and selected a flashing screen crafted for music. Pictures of snow-covered forests and cozy homes with lights in the windows flashed slowly across the screen while someone chirped about walking in a winter wonderland.

Chirped…

"Oh," he groaned as Emily tugged a bushy stick of metal out of the narrow tree box.

"What's wrong?" she asked with a frown.

"These chirping creatures… Are they trapped? I freed some…" He smacked his forehead when he realized what he'd done.

"Oh, I bet you mean at the spaceport?" Her face cleared. "Now I understand what happened. Aw, honey." After lowering the bushy metal stalk to the floor, she crossed around the table of coff-ee and gave Likir a hug he had no idea he needed but was grateful to receive. "You thought there were creatures singing inside the PA system?"

"I feel foolish."

"The music you hear on the TV was recorded to be played whenever someone chooses it. At the spaceport, they were piping the music in through the boxes on the ceiling."

He cringed. "Ugh." Her word, but he liked using it. "I destroyed property."

"I assume you thought you were rescuing the creatures trapped in the box."

He nodded. "I must repair these PA boxes at the spaceport."

"I'm sure they've taken care of it already. For all we know, you're not the first Cu'zod to do this."

He didn't believe that, but he was grateful for her understanding and kind words. And her hug. He wanted to receive those every day of his life.

Her shining face beamed up at him, and he couldn't resist tasting her mouth.

She moaned and pressed closer before leaning back. Her finger rose between them, and she wiggled it in the air. "None of that, now, though I'd be happy to kiss you all evening. We have a tree to set up and decorate and then the mall awaits."

He wasn't sure about this mall, but if it gave him more time with Emily, he would follow her wherever she led.

Pretend was starting to turn real. How long would this last?

13

Emily

"I am not sure this looks like a tree," Likir said, sounding completely diplomatic. If his lower lip wasn't shaking, she'd be more apt to believe him. "It is silver. I have not seen silver trees here on Earth."

She giggled. Her, the normally stoic person, actually giggled. "I know silver isn't the usual Earth tree color, but it's still pretty, isn't it?"

Alfred bounced around the tree, leaping up to grab the lower branches with his teeth. She scooped him into her arms and showed him the tree from her angle.

Likir did the same with Valicia, who'd taken to riding on his shoulder whenever she could. Like with Alfred, Emily had a feeling Valicia would be remaining permanently at the rescue. Or for as long as Likir was here.

She didn't want to think about him leaving.

She and Likir had decked the tree with red and green balls and strands of white lights, just the way her grannie had done when she was alive.

"It's an old tree," Emily said, tugging on a limb.

"I did notice dust on the box."

"Grannie got it in the eighties. As long as I put this tree up and use these decorations, I feel like she's still with me."

His arms went around her from behind, and he kissed her neck. "It is beautiful."

"It is kind of silly to cling to something like this, though, isn't it? For some reason, I can't let it go."

"It shows you care. And I… I am slowly starting to see its beauty."

"I guess the saying is right, beauty is in the eye of the beholder. To me, this is the prettiest thing I've ever seen."

Was putting up this tree truly showing Likir the meaning of Christmas, however? Emily wasn't sure.

"They say Christmas lives in your heart," she said. "That it's not about pretty decorations or presents or eating tons of expensive food. It's about family, love, and a touch of holiday magic. I hope my tree keeps giving me a happy feeling whenever I see it."

"Viewing it through your eyes makes it lovely to me."

"Thank you." Wiping her eyes, she faced him. "It's still early. Let's go to the mall and get the material we need to make our costumes. While we're there, I'll show you a bit more of the meaning of Christmas."

While he went upstairs to retrieve something, she stuffed her feet into her boots and donned her winterwear. She started her car to warm it up. Then she loaded Alfred in his sling carrier.

Not long later, they climbed inside her car and buckled up. She wondered if he'd be nervous about riding with her again, but he didn't appear to be so far.

"Would you mind holding Alfred?" she asked, unclipping the carrier.

"Of course not." He settled the pup on his lap and stared out the window. "What exactly is a mall?"

"It's a cluster of stores within one building."

She backed down her drive and pulled out onto the road, keeping her speed well below the limit as she drove.

The mall was on the other side of town, and since it was starting to get dark, she decided to take the vehicle through the fancier area where the owners had decorated their homes and lawns.

"This is incredible," he said, gaping out the window. "So many lights."

"It's a bit commercialized," she said, an understatement.

"But there is beauty in it. Look how the trees glow. I imagine they are pleased to have people looking at them."

She hadn't thought of the trees, more of the inflatable Santa's and snowmen bobbing in the wind on the lawns.

"And look at the small striplings walking with their parents," he said, pointing. "They see the magic."

"They do. You're right."

Perhaps he was discovering the meaning of Christmas after all.

14

Likir

"*M*alls are the third cavern of heila," Likir said, gritting his fangs together. People. So many people! And sounds, a cacophony that never ended. Music, voices, and bangs. He almost couldn't bear it.

"I take it the third cavern of heila isn't a good place to be," Emily said, walking at his side. They wove through the crowds, passing one lit-up store after another. People gawked, pointed, and some staggered backward when they saw him. This, he expected. The stimulation? Not at all.

"Third cavern of heila is the place where those who harm others go when they die. A brave warrior who finds ways to do good in their life is taken by the lunarsprite beyond the three moons of Cu'zod to find their final resting place."

"Ah." Humor bubbled within her voice, but she kept her tone neutral. He appreciated that. "I don't disagree with you, then. This place is heilish."

"So many people," he grunted.

"It's crowded, isn't it?" Emily shot him a concerned

look. One of her hands held his tightly, as if she thought he'd bolt.

She wasn't wrong in that assumption. The urge nearly drowned him.

Her other hand rested on the sack holding Alfred against her chest.

"We won't be here long," she said. "Why don't we hurry to the craft store and then we can scoot out of here?"

"You said you wished to show me something here that defines Christmas." He would bear this torture to see such an event.

"I could show you in other ways."

"We will obtain the ingredients for this cost-oom, witness the event, then flee this cavern of heila."

"I know it's a cliché, but most guys don't enjoy shopping. Maybe you're like them?"

"Perhaps." He didn't believe his feelings had anything to do with him being male versus female.

She led him into a colorful place of commerce and the crowd thinned somewhat, taken over by rows of merchandise and a few humans pushing metal carts loaded with various goods.

His tension level dropped.

"I think felt will work best," she said, tapping her chin. "Red and green. And I'll get some glue sticks since my gun is out. Oh, and bells. And glitter glue. They probably have patterns, too, though I'm not sure any will be big enough for you."

She hurried to the back of the place of commerce, pushing her own metal cart, and he followed, carrying Alfred for her. The little guy kept poking his head out and sniffing the air.

Something did smell delicious here. Was it the felt? If

not, could he talk Emily into seeking out the source of this smell once they had purchased the goods needed to turn them both into elves?

She consulted with a female standing behind a counter, who gaped at Likir. He grinned, showing his fangs, and her eyes widened further. She backed away from the counter before her entire body shook. With a stiffening spine, she rounded the counter and led them further into the back of this place of commerce, where she sliced through large pieces of red and green fuzzy flats. They were folded and scraps of paper stapled to them. As Emily named the goods she wished to purchase, the female brought them to bags of silver balls dangling from racks on the ends of the aisle that made a jingling sound when touched.

"I think that's all you'll need," the female said, frowning. Her gaze glided to Likir's feet. "I recommend using black felt to make elf shoes; perhaps a covering for sneakers?"

"Great idea," Emily said. "Do you know where we might find red and white striped tights?"

"I bet you can find white ones at the department store." The female's gaze fell on Likir again. "Maybe attach red strips of sparkly cloth or red glitter glue? Try plus sized tights for him. They'll stretch up rather than out."

Tights… His translator gave him a definition—a thin, close-fitting garment, typically made of nylon or other knitted yarn, covering the legs, hips, and bottom.

"Red and white tights, you say?" he asked, curious to see how this would look stretched over his legs.

"We'll wear them as part of our costume." Emily clapped her hands, and he was caught up in her enthusiasm. "These costumes are going to be amazing."

"Others will dress like this at the ball?" he asked as they

left the place of commerce with bags containing their purchases.

"Not only elves. Some will dress as reindeer or snowman. A bunch of Santa's, I bet, too. We're going to schmooze and find donors who will support the rescue." Stopping in the middle of the path, Emily paused to nuzzle Alfred. Alfred wiggled, delivering doo-gee kisses. "They're going to be so eager to support our rescue that they'll fling cash my way." She grinned up at Likir. "Let's get those tights, shall we?"

He was following her toward the dee-part-ment store when the scent he'd caught earlier reached his senses again. He stopped, and someone bumped into his back.

The person snarled. "Jeez, dude, watch..."

When Likir turned, one brow lifted and his tail coiled up onto his shoulder, the person stumbled backward.

"You're one of those... Whoa." The older stripling darted around Likir and raced forward, shooting looks over his shoulder.

"It's an alien," someone else cried. "So freakin' cool!"

Emily took his hand. "Act natural."

"How else could I act other than by my usual nature?" he asked, puzzled.

"Keep walking or we'll be mobbed. Quick question. Have you ever given autographs?"

Auto...?

"Not so far," he said.

"Hopefully, we'll avoid a gathering crowd and a signing."

He would prefer this, too. Perhaps if they left the main section of the mall, they'd draw less attention.

"Can you help me find that unusual scent?" he asked, another worthy distraction.

"Scent?" Stopping, she sniffed the air and grinned.

"Okay, so maybe you'll enjoy this before we finish our descent into the third cavern of heila."

"What has created the delicious smell?"

"Only one of the best Christmas things in the world." She leaned into his side and looked up at him, her eyes sparkling. "How would you like to frost your own gingerbread cookie?"

"I would like this very much." He had no idea what a frost or gingerbread cookie was, but surely this amazing smell would only lead him to something wonderful.

"Then it's time to enter the winter wonderland," she said.

"I have heard the voices on the tee-vee singing about this wonderland."

"Walking in a winter wonderland," Emily sang.

Someone passing them from the opposite direction smiled and joined in with Emily, singing the song.

They walked to the middle of the wings of commerce, approaching a wonderous land unlike anything Likir had seen before. Huge white boulders were surrounded by green trees covered with white lights and red balls. Overhead, music chirped about bells jingling, and he marveled that such a thing was possible. So much of Earth was pretend, much like how he and Emily had started their relationship. Perhaps this pretend Christmas would also bring him further joy and help him transition to something bigger with Emily.

"A lot of the activities here are for little kids, but we're kids a heart, right?" Emily said, leading him over to a big glass-coated case with an older stripling standing behind it dressed in a red and white striped garment. "Do you want a boy or girl?"

"Excuse me?" He looked around, wondering what she meant, and caught Stanley, his elder friend, looking their way. Stanley waved and leaned over a female stripling sitting at a round table, a bottle of green liquid in her hand.

"Do you want to frost a boy or girl cookie?" Emily said, explaining.

"Ah, the source of this amazing scent are these coo-kees." He leaned closer to the glass, taking in the rows of brown, being-shaped objects. "Both?"

She laughed. "Sure, why not?" She spoke to the older stripling standing behind the glass cabinet and the stripling handed Emily plates containing the coo-kees, taking Emily's flat card in exchange.

After her card was returned, Emily nudged her head toward an empty table near Stanley's "Let's frost these babies!"

At Likir's nod, she carried the plates with brown, flat bodies to the table. Bottles of colorful liquid waited in the center, on a small tray. Emily slid the plate holding his boy and girl coo-kees in front of him, keeping the plate with a male coo-kee for herself.

"Now we squirt them with frosting," she said.

"What is frosting?" he asked.

"You're going to be amazed."

Everything on Earth was amazing to him, but mostly Emily. He enjoyed being her friendly boy. He wanted it to be real for always, though, and not pretend.

Stanley winked at Likir, who winked back.

Emily upended one of the bottles and dumped light green liquid onto her coo-kee. Likir did the same with pale red and white, coating each coo-kee's surface.

"What will we do with the coo-kees?" he asked when they were completely coated.

"Eat them," she said as if it was perfectly clear. Lifting her boy coo-kee, she bit off a leg, closing her eyes and wiggling while she chewed. Her eyes opened. "Aren't you going to try yours?"

Actually, he wanted to lick the green frosting off her lips even if it tasted horrible but would have to settle for one of his coo-kees. Lifting it, he stared down his nose at the murky, gleaming surface covering the brown.

How could this thing be the source of the unbelievable smell?

Emily gyrated in place while savoring each morsel of her coo-kee. If she enjoyed it, he would, too, correct?

He took a bite and chewed slowly.

"What do you think?" Emily asked, watching him.

So sweet. He'd never tasted anything like this before. The frosting melted, gliding across his tongue, and the coo-kee beneath carried an odd, yet appealing, flavor. Bread of the ginger, Emily had called it? He couldn't be sure.

Perhaps replicators were not the best way of obtaining food.

"I love this coo-kee," he said. "It is—"

"Well, well, well," someone drawled behind them. Likir turned to find Emily's ex standing nearby with a female clinging to his side. "If it isn't Emily with her... What did you call yourself, Cu'zod? Ah, yes, her friendly boy." He snickered and the female with him giggled, a high-pitched sound that grated on Likir's nerves.

"Go away, Bradley," Emily said, taking another bite of her coo-kee. "We're busy."

"I want those tickets back."

Emily's eyes popped. "You said I could have them if I had a date." Her arm linked through Likir's. "You remember Likir, don't you? He's my date."

The female with Brad-lee stared at Likir, her mouth ajar. "That's an alien, Bradley."

Brad-lee's eyes rolled around in his head. "What gave you that idea, Bridget?"

Bridget stepped forward, leaving Brad-lee. "Are you from Cu'zod?"

"I am," Likir said. He lowered the rest of his coo-kee to the plate as the female strolled around him, studying him from every angle.

"Do you have scales all over your body?" she asked. "Because that's really cool."

"Bridget," Emily huffed. "Didn't your parents teach you any manners?"

"Sure, they did, but then I grew up." Bridget flashed Likir a smile. "You look familiar, for some reason."

"Perhaps because you have seen other Cu'zods on the tee-vee?" Likir said.

"That could be it, but…" Her head tilted as she studied his face. "I could swear it's more than that. Are you famous?"

His gaze shot to Emily, and she shrugged.

"I am not famous," he said. "I am a regular Cu'zod warrior."

"Warrior?" Bridget said while Brad-lee grumbled something about his friendly girl checking the out of another male.

Under normal circumstances, Likir might flash his fangs Bridget's way, solely to irritate Brad-lee, but Emily was with him, and all his fang flashes belonged to her.

Likir stood and dipped forward in a bow. "I have trained in a variety of fighting techniques."

"Like, with a sword?" she gushed. "I love watching sword battles in movies."

Emily sighed. "We were having cookies."

"See, now that's where I'm confused," Brad-lee said, coming closer.

"How so?" Emily asked. She nibbled on her coo-kee, and all Likir could see was those same teeth nibbling on his cock. Her lips—

"You say this Cu'zod is your boyfriend," Brad-lee said.

She grinned, sharing a conspiratorial smile with Likir. "He is."

"Yet that's forbidden. I would've thought if anyone was about following the rules, it would be you, Emily."

The rest of her coo-kee fell from her hand. It hit the edge of the table and plunged to the floor, landing frosting-side down. "Spit it out, Bradley."

Likir waited for more nasty words to project from Brad-lee's mouth like spit. Such an amazing term, spitting it out. Unfortunately, Likir had a feeling whatever words Brad-lee spit would hit them in an equally unpleasant way.

"I was talking with my golf partner, Michael Sussix," Brad-lee said. "You remember him, don't you, Emily?"

"Say it," she whispered. Tears filled her eyes, and she sent a look of panic Likir's way.

"Michael was telling me a bit more about the Cu'zod sponsorship program. It seems there's one little rule you're ignoring that could land you in jail, Emily."

She stood so fast; her chair rocked backward, nearly falling over. "What are you talking about?"

"One of the rules states no fraternizing with those you sponsor." Bradley sneered while Bridget frowned. "You're not allowed to date this Cu'zod *warrior*."

15

Emily

"I'll come by for the tickets tomorrow evening, Emily," Bradley said, his voice grating on her nerves. "Please have them ready. If you hand them over without protest, I'll overlook this..." His sneer turned to Likir. "*Thing* you're dating."

"He's not a thing," Emily roared, storming up to Bradley.

He pushed her away.

Likir's growl rumbled around them, and his tail whipped out, encircling Bradley's neck, tightening until Bradley's face was ruddier than a tomato.

He clawed at Likir's tail, sputtering.

Emily backed away from Bradley, into Likir's arms. "Let him go. He's not worth getting into trouble over."

Likir's tail snapped back, and he eased Emily to the side, stepping in front of her.

"Do not touch Emily again," he snarled, his fangs gnashing. With fury on his face and the spikes on the top of his head raised, he was a formidable opponent.

Bradley stumbled backward, his hands raising. "You

think I won't report this to the authorities? You can't threaten me and get away with it. One word from me to Michael, and you'll be on a ship back to Cu'zod so fast, your head will spin."

Emily's heart thudded like elephants ran through her chest, and her hands went clammy. "I'll give you the tickets," she said in desperation. "Just let this go. Please?" She didn't care about herself; she couldn't bear it if Likir was sent back.

Bradley tugged on his coat, smoothing the fabric. "Give me the tickets and I'll…think about not calling Michael."

Utter defeat filled Emily. Without the tickets, she couldn't go to the ball. Without that opportunity, she'd lose her business. Everything was falling apart, and there was nothing she could do about it. "Come by tomorrow, after dinner, and I'll hand them over."

As important as the ball might be, Likir mattered more. If he was sent back to Cu'zod, she'd never see him again, and her heart seized at the thought.

Bradley huffed. His attention fell on Bridget, and he growled. "Let's go."

"But Bradley," Bridget said, nearly salivating as she stared at Likir's abandoned gingerbread couple. "You said we were going to paint cookies."

"You don't need one." Bradley pivoted on his heel and started striding away. "Come on!"

Bridget sighed.

"Girl, I'd get out of that so fast, my head would spin," Emily said in a low voice. "You can see what he's like, can't you? Such an asshole. Don't wait until you hear about his cheating from other women, like I did."

"He…cheated on you?" Bridget said with a frown that took in Bradley striding toward Hot Topic.

"In the year I was with him he cheated on me with four women."

"Ugh," Bridget said. "He's got money, he's hot, and… Fuck. I'm not sure all that matters if he's slime." She started following after Bradley but turned. "Thanks. You've given me something to think about."

Emily had probably just given Bradley another reason to be angry, but Bridget seemed like a decent person. She deserved better.

Every woman deserved better.

"I am sorry," Likir said, his arms going around Emily from behind. "I should not have assaulted Brad-lee."

"He deserves it. He's a jerk, and I hope bad things happen to him." She heaved out a sigh. "Well, maybe not horribly bad things. Just sorta bad things. I'm not mean."

He kissed the top of her head. "I did not know about this rule regarding relationships."

It was going to be a problem. Unfortunately, it made sense that a host would not get involved with the Cu'zod they sponsored. It could cross the line.

But love didn't obey rules.

Love?

She pinched her eyes shut. It wasn't clear if she loved Likir yet, but she could tell she was starting to fall already.

"This rule needs to be eliminated," he said.

"I'm not sure how." She turned in his embrace, looking up at him. To think she could lose him even sooner than she'd thought. He'd barely come into her life, and she would be forced to either send him to another sponsor or end what they'd recently gotten started. "I don't have the power to do anything like that, do you?"

Shadows chased across his face, and for a second, she worried he was hiding something from her.

He wouldn't do something like that. He knew Bradley hurt her when he lied.

Likir was nothing like Bradley.

"I don't think anyone can change the rules," she said, stepping out of his embrace. No need to give observers fodder. Bradley wasn't the only one who could report them.

Why hadn't she read the fine print in the paperwork? Because she was excited. And she never thought she'd come to care for the Cu'zod she would help transition into a new life on Earth.

"Do you want the rest of your cookies?" she asked. Hers had fallen onto the floor, and she wouldn't be replacing it. Her belly churned; her appetite fled.

"I am finished. Perhaps I can wrap them and take them home? We might wish to eat them later."

Right now, the thought of food made her nauseous.

Despite the horrifying situation, she felt bad. She'd come here not just to buy material for their elf costumes but to show Likir how wonderful Christmas was. If she was in school, she'd have an F on that project.

There was one thing she could do before they left the mall, however…

16

Likir

"Why do we wait in line with striplings?" Likir said.

"You'll see. It's fun," she said with what he could tell was forced humor. She was doing her best to make this entertaining for him, despite her own dismay.

How could he tell her that while he'd set aside his royal status, he still could ask for almost anything he wanted here, and it would be granted?

This simple rule meant nothing. A flick of his hand, plus a quick discussion with Trex, his friend who was now the Ambassador of Cu'zod, and the rule would go away.

But Emily had been hurt when Brad-lee used his wealth and power to manipulate her. He was still doing so.

Likir did not wish to appear as if he was as manipulative as Brad-lee. When Likir came to Earth, he was determined to live like every other Cu'zod immigrant. He refused to fall back on the power his family wielded, power that was given to him solely by the name he was born into, not because he'd earned it.

He would have to discover a way out of this tenuous

situation, because he refused to let Emily go. And he wanted to continue working at the rescue with her. He loved this job and the animals.

"This is just one way we share Christmas," Emily said, her face tense with a frown. A soft light shone in her eyes. She wanted to do this for him. How could he deny her?

"Standing in line is a Christmas activity?" he asked, still skeptical.

"Ha, ha," she said, wrapping her arm through his and leaning her head against his shoulder. "Funny."

He wasn't being humorous, was he?

Perhaps it would be best to go along with this and see where it ended. It must be one of the magical parts of this Earth holiday Emily enjoyed, and who was he to step aside and not experience it fully?

"It looks like a long line, but it'll go fast." Emily stood on her toes, scanning the line ahead of them winding into a tall, white-covered mound structure. Someone ahead kept shouting *ho, ho, ho*, but he couldn't see who the being yet to identify him. "See? One of the elves just took a few kids back."

Ah, yes, there was a female dressed in an elf costume escorting a stripling behind the white mounds.

"Hey, do you mind if I run to the rest room while you hold our place in line?" Emily asked.

"You need to rest?"

"Well, no, it's actually a bathroom."

"You need to bathe?" he teased, knowing very well what she meant. But he hated to see her so distressed with no way in sight to fix it.

She sighed, though she looked more like she wanted to laugh than frown. "I need to go…" Her voice lowered. "Pee."

"Then why not call it a pee room?"

A stripling nearby laughed. "Mommy, I gotta go to the pee room."

"Honey, we don't call it that," the mother said, her wide gaze locked on Likir.

"But he did!" The stripling's finger poked toward Likir.

He dipped his head forward. "I am sorry."

"Thanks." Emily hugged his arm. "I'll be right back?"

"Of course."

She scooted away, crossing the big open space in the center of the commerce building and entering a hall that he presumed led to the rest-bath-pee room.

The line shifted forward, and he moved with it. A few of the elders herding striplings gawked at Likir, but he was becoming used to this. He was a visitor from another planet. If his scales, tail, and horns weren't remarked upon, they pointed to the spikes jutting across the top of his head.

He was also aware of how Earthlings had viewed "aliens" for many generations. Little green men. He'd laughed when he heard this, as he was blue and hardly little, even for a Cu'zod.

"I couldn't help but overhear," a voice said from behind him.

Likir turned to find his friend, Stanley, standing beyond the edge of the line. When their gazes met, Stanley stepped forward, holding out his hand. "I'd like to give these to you. They send me two every year, as I'm a member of the club, but I never have any use for them. I'm more of a homebody." He frowned. "Bah, humbug, right?" His chuckle rang out. "Not really. I just prefer smaller, more intimate family gatherings."

Likir took the rectangular paper object from Stanley, unsure what it could be.

Stanley's gaze took in the line, and he chuckled. "I've

already been to see Santa, and now it's time for a bit more shopping. I'll see you later?"

"Yes, of course," Likir said. "And thank you?" Although, he wasn't sure yet what he was thanking Stanley for.

He tucked the white rectangle into his pocket to examine later.

Emily returned.

"Almost there," she said, standing on her toes to scan the line. "I can't wait to share this with you."

"I am sure I will be amazed."

Tiny Earthlings surrounded them. Some bounced and squealed. Others teased smaller striplings clinging to elder's hands.

Still others wept.

"How can something that creates sadness in a stripling show the meaning of Christmas?" he asked, truly curious to hear her answer.

"It's fun." Her face knotted. "Well, it is once they reach Santa."

"Ah yes, Santa." He craned his neck forward, but was unable to find the round, red and white dressed male everyone seemed to revere. This male featured in almost every Christmas moo-vee they'd watched on the tee-vee.

"We're going to meet him," she said with a laugh. "You'll love it."

This, he had to see.

They slowly worked their way forward and eventually, they stood in front of the female elf.

She gaped up at him. "He's not a little kid. Neither are you."

"I know, but he's new to Earth, and he wants to meet Santa," Emily said. "I don't need to, but he does."

She bobbed her head. "He's one of those Cu'zod warriors, right?"

Likir bowed. "I am."

The female elf lifted her eyebrows. He liked her clothing and looked forward to wearing the matching set he and Emily would craft for them. Oh, wait, Bradley was going to take the tee-kets which meant they would not be attending the ball.

Unless Likir could find a way for them to go. Was it permissible to go without tee-kets?

If not, he could speak to Trex about this. Surely, he could arrange for tee-kets to "magically" appear at Emily's dwelling. This would be seen as part of the wonder of this holiday, would it not?

"I will not speak long with Santa," Likir told the elf.

"All right," she said with a soft laugh. "I guess there's no harm in it. But you have to be quick. Little kids are waiting." Spinning her eyes, she held her hand out to Likir. "Come on. Let's lead you up to Santa, big buddy."

Emily grinned, and that was all Likir needed to feel complete.

The real wonder of Christmas was in her smile. The warmth in her eyes. Her hand soft on his spine as she followed him.

"Up here," the female elf said. She directed them around the huge mounds of snow that was not cold like it was outside, large red and white striped hooks embedded in the not-cold snow, and then up a short flight of stairs leading to a platform. More snow that wasn't cold awaited them, as did a huge, golden chair and...

"Santa," Likir breathed, staring at amazement at the male dressed in a red and white costume.

"Please don't tell me you're going to sit on his lap," the female elf said.

"I do not believe I will," Likir said.

Emily giggled, though a touch of nervousness crept into her tone. "You don't need to sit on his lap. When kids meet Santa at times like this, they tell him what they want for Christmas. You can do that while standing beside him."

He already knew what he wanted for Christmas: Emily. It wasn't that simple, however. Asking a male dressed in red and white to grant his wish would not make it come true.

But the wonder of Christmas suggested it could.

He had to try.

"Right this way, big kid," the female elf said. She hustled him and Emily across the platform. They followed a stripling in a bright red dress.

The stripling sobbed against her mother's leg. "Don't wanna. Don't wanna!"

"Come now, Cara. It's Santa! You've been excited to meet him for months." The harried mother glanced their way. She blinked a few times and rubbed her eyes. "You're one of those aliens."

"Likir Thuzok," he said with a short bow.

"Why are you in the line for Santa?"

"How else will I get what I wish for?"

She snickered. "You're right. Let's all sit on Santa's lap and ask for things. Personally, I'd love one of those four-door Jeeps. How about you?"

Emily. He wanted Emily.

"I have many wishes," he said.

"I'm sure you do." The female nudged her stripling forward. "Come on, Cara, it's your turn."

"Don't wanna!"

The mother tugged Cara over to the male dressed in red and white who sat on the golden chair. Santa looked as harried as the mother, and…

"He is not real," Likir said softly, somewhat disappointed.

"Of course he is," Emily said in complete seriousness. "He is if you believe in your heart."

Could Likir let go and let belief carry him through this?

As he was hurried forward to meet "Santa," he decided he could try.

Or he could become his own version of Santa and make the wonder of Christmas happen for Emily.

17

Emily

As she drove home, Emily tried to keep her spirits up. But now that the supposed "magic" of Christmas was left behind, she couldn't hold onto the feeling.

Bradley seemed determined to ruin her, though she didn't know why. He was the one who cheated.

She did give him the final push out the door, but he was halfway out already. Perhaps that was it. He didn't have the final say, and he didn't like that. That could be why he kept trying to taunt her with Bridget. As if she cared he was with yet another woman? Once she found out he was a cheater, she was finished with him. Her feelings for him shriveled like the wicked witch doused with water in the Wizard of Oz.

"After we've taken the dogs for a walk," Emily said as she drove down Main Street, "and fed everyone, plus tidied the pens, we need to talk about everything." About what they would do.

"All right." His gaze turned, and he stared out the window. "The lights are pretty."

They blazed for all to see, but the gorgeous lights were a façade, at least for Emily. "I'm sorry it's come to this. I didn't know about the rule or I…"

"Could we have stopped it?" Honesty grated in his voice. "I do not believe I could have. I…care for you, Emily. Very much."

"I feel the same." A crack widened in her heart, and she knew if he left, the opening would never heal over.

"I did not know of this rule either." Shadows chased across his face in the fading light. The sun had set and while the streetlights guided Emily home, they weren't bright enough to read his expression. "I am also sorry. I do not wish to get you in trouble with the authorities."

She pulled into her drive and shut off the car.

"They'll take you from me." It wasn't about her, though she couldn't stop the pain from flooding through her chest, squeezing it so tight she couldn't breathe. "It's not about your work at the rescue, you know that." Taking his hand, she held it, feeling as if he'd be wrenched from her soon. "We've started something that…"

"Something we may not be allowed to finish."

"I don't want to endanger your chance on Earth." She'd push him away if it would give him the opportunity he'd sought when he came here.

"I don't want to leave Earth, but even more, I don't want to leave you."

There didn't seem to be a way around this.

The pretty lights she'd showed Likir earlier seemed dull now that their future was uncertain. At least when she had tickets to the ball and him by her side, she had hope that something good might happen.

Now she faced a new dilemma.

"Bradley isn't the type of person to take the tickets back and let this go," she said, gnawing on a fingernail. "As he said, if I don't hand them over, he'll have Michael on the phone within seconds. He'll tell Michael we're dating, and the government will intervene."

"Why does he do this?" Likir turned to her, studying her face in the dim driveway light. "He is relentless."

"Because he's determined to ruin my life. He doesn't want me happy for whatever reason. He saw us having fun, and he wants to take that away."

"He has a new female in his life. Why pursue this with you when it would be easier to walk in the opposite direction?"

"Because I was the one to end it. I discovered he was cheating on me with others, and I told him to leave. That's not Bradley's way. He's the one to end things. He told me that once."

"This is about revenge for what he perceives as a slight?"

"Yes. It's as simple as that." There was no winning with someone like that. He held all the power, and he'd use it against her. Ruin her, then he'd cackle as he took Likir down along with her.

They got out of the car and went inside, flopping onto the sofa side by side. She released Alfred from his pouch, and he scampered into the kitchen to check out the food bowl she needed to fill.

Likir tugged her up onto his lap and held her close.

Emily stared at the pretty Christmas lights on her grandmother's tree and couldn't find the spark of joy from earlier. Grannie's magic didn't seem to be working any longer.

Her vision shimmered as tears fell down her face unchecked.

"If it was just about the tickets to the ball, I'd hand

them over without question," she said through her sniffles. "But I know Bradley. He'll take the tickets, no doubt about that. Then he'll still call Michael. He won't stop until he's turned me into a weeping wreck."

Likir's arms tightened around her. "I will not let him do this. There has to be a way to keep him from winning."

"Don't you see? This isn't about winning. It was about being a humane person. The animals will suffer most, and Bradley won't care about that as long as I'm hurt."

Likir snarled, and she knew he'd rip the other man apart if Bradley walked through the door right now. She couldn't have that; such action would result in him being banished from Earth forever.

"At best, we have a day or two before someone shows up and insists you leave," she said. No, insists they take him from her life. If they were lucky, he'd be allowed to remain on Earth.

"Then we need to make the best of the time we have. After that, we'll find a way."

She loved that he could make this vow, but how would that ever happen? They wouldn't just take him from her life, they'd likely send him far away from her.

Breaking the rules could come with a monetary or legal punishment, for all she knew. If she went to jail, everything would fall apart. The horror of that thought crashed through her, but despite how scary it might be, it was worse knowing she might never see Likir again.

So much for showing him the wonder of Christmas. It had turned into a horror show.

But wait, it didn't have to. Bradley hadn't done anything yet. She doubted he'd called Michael. He wouldn't use that weapon against her until he could watch her pain while it unfolded in front of her.

They had now. At best, tonight, and until Bradley came to her house tomorrow.

It was time to make the best of it.

"I'm going to get into my PJs, and we can finish putting out decorations," she said. Doing something normal would ground her and somehow, maybe make this short time together better.

Tonight? No more sleeping alone in the guest bed.

She rose and scooted upstairs while he removed his boots.

When she returned downstairs in her adult footie PJs she'd picked up as a joke but now adored, Likir stood in the middle of the living room, a huge smile on his face.

"I believe I've found a way to show the wonder of Christmas," he said, his hand outstretched toward her. An open envelope sat on his palm.

"What's this?" she asked, taking it from him.

"Open and you will see." His fangs flashed, and like always, the heat in his gaze burned through her. Definitely needed to find her way back into the king bed tonight.

She opened the envelope and gaped down at what lay in her hands. "How is this possible?" A glance to the entry table showed Bradley's tickets to the ball still sitting where she'd left them.

How then, did she hold another pair of tickets?

"The wonder of Christmas has delivered," Likir said.

Never knock a gift horse in the mouth, Grannie always said. Who cared where Likir got them? He had, and they gave her a chance to save Christmas for the animals in her rescue even if she couldn't save it for her and Likir.

For the first time since Bradley showed up at the mall, Emily smiled.

Tonight would be theirs. Tomorrow too.

But for now, the magic of the ball awaited them.

She scooted forward, into Likir's open arms, and looked up at him. "I think it's time to make some elf costumes."

18

Likir

"Let's spread the felt out on the kitchen table," Emily said. "We can cut it out there and then use Grannie's sewing machine to stitch it together."

Shadows lurked in her eyes, and they must have been in his, too. A feeling of desperation filled him. He wanted so much with her, but it wasn't solely about them being together.

He enjoyed his job here at the rescue. He loved watching timid creatures bloom before his eyes. They learned to trust and gave incredible love once they found someone they knew would not harm them.

Alfred hopped into the kitchen, joining them with his tongue lolling and his big eyes sparkling. Valicia scampered after him, leaping to grab his stubby tail.

"We should make Alfred a costume, too," Likir said. "He can go to the ball with us."

"What a fantastic idea," she said. "I bet we could sneak him into the event if he's dressed, too. He's the best salesman I've got."

It was clear she was pushing to remain cheerful. If she could do this, Likir could too.

She cleared the kitchen table then spread out the green material. After tacking the pattern pieces onto the surface, she cut. Many snips later, and the big piece was gone, replaced by small bits that would somehow turn him and Emily into elves.

"Follow me," she said with a smile, leading him upstairs to her guest bedroom. She placed the pile of cut pieces on her bed and unveiled a metal object sitting on a table beneath a printed cloth. "This is Grannie's sewing machine." She pulled a chair away from the table. "It's going to take me awhile to sew everything together."

"Can I help?"

"We only have one machine, but there's a task you can do." She lifted several small bags that jingled, tempting him to say ho, ho, ho. "Once the tops and hats are assembled, you can start sewing on bells."

"Why don't I collect Valicia to help with this task?"

She chuckled. "That sounds like a wonderful idea. She'll love chasing the balls around the room."

While she sat and the machine whirred, he went downstairs and found Valicia snuggled in the doo-gee bed with Alfred. She mewed when she saw him, clambering up his pants.

Such a tiny, amazing creature. Her claws were sharp, and her tiny teeth pricked, but when she rumbled in her fuzzy throat and rubbed her head against Likir's face, his heart essentially broke.

He took Valicia up to Emily's room, where he sat on the floor with the first constructed hat, the bells, and sueing materials. Valicia watched curiously from his shoulder.

"You are sure this sharp object with this three-d will hold the jingles in place?" he asked as Valicia crawled down his arm to investigate the strand of green three-d. She batted it when he held it up to show Emily.

"It will. Sew it on tight then add a few extra stitches, and it'll hold. We won't be tugging on them."

He wasn't sure, but he trusted Emily. Valicia helped him sew the first jingle onto the hat, a large red one that would crown the top. Despite the kee-ten climbing the back of his shirt and perching on top of his head, he was able to affix the big jingles to both hats.

He tugged a completed tunic close and started adding smaller jingles to the collar. Other big ones would be affixed to the shoe coverings.

They worked into the evening as there were only a few days left until the Christmas Costume Ball, and they wanted to be ready.

"Done," Emily said, scooting her chair away from the sue-ing machine hours later. "The last pants." She held them up and grinned. "Yours. How goes the bell attachment operation?"

His fingers stung from being pricked, and it was a challenge doing this task with Valicia slumbering on his lap, but he was also done. The teets—tights—lay beside him, white material with red glitter stripes. He held up Emily's tunic, a green, red, and white thing with red and white striped sleeves. "Finished."

"Perfect," she said. "Now we should try them on, don't you think?"

He was excited about this. This costume... He'd never seen anything like it. But the female elf at the mall wore one, though this was much more intricate. Hers had consisted of a collar over a red shirt and a green skirt worn over her blue pants. A hat on her head made her a decent elf, but these costumes were amazing.

"You have done an unbelievable job," he said, carefully

lowering Valicia onto a blanket lying on the floor nearby. She wiggled, stretching out her tiny legs and curling her pin-prick claws.

"I couldn't have done it without you." Emily dropped down onto his lap and wrapped her arms around him. He wished they could remain like this forever.

She was right, what they had was going to end, and he couldn't see how it would finish except badly. They were both going to be hurt, and there was no way out.

But it wasn't over yet. They might still be able to steal a little Christmas magic for each other.

"Yes," he said, rising. "Let us try on our elf costumes."

She climbed off his lap and faced him, a soft smile on her face.

Her grin widened, and she tugged her shirt up and over her head. She tossed it aside and reached for her pants.

His cock flared, eager to discover what it was denied days ago.

"Emily…" he said hoarsely. "If we continue in this way, we will not be trying on our costumes."

"Maybe our costumes can wait until tomorrow?"

Flames licked up his spine, and the spikes on the top of his head went equally rigid. "Are you sure?"

Biting her lower lip, she nodded. Her gaze fell on Valicia. "I'm sure she'll be fine here alone for a bit."

"It may be a long bite—*bit*."

"Then perhaps we should return her to her crate?"

He carefully scooped her up and raced to the animal area, his footsteps heavy on the stairs. Emily's merry laughter followed him, driving him on.

The sleepy kee-ten barely stirred as he lowered her onto the soft pile of cloths inside the cage. She curled up, purring as he carefully closed the latch.

When he returned to the second story of Emily's dwelling, he found her standing outside the bedroom he'd used—*her* room. Her scent had haunted him these past nights.

She wore nothing, and she was the most beautiful sight he'd ever seen.

He practically ripped through his clothing with his claws to remove it.

She watched, the tip of her pink tongue that could deliver incredible pleasure poking past her lips.

He stalked toward her, completely naked, with his cock blazing for her to see and scooped her up. He buried his face in her neck, nipping at her soft flesh with his fangs.

"I want you," he growled.

Her smoldering gaze met his, and heat blazed in her voice. "Then take me."

19

Emily

Likir carried Emily into her former bedroom—*their* bedroom from now on if she had any say in it. Skin against scales felt amazing, a slightly rough yet strangely smooth rubbing of one body against the other.

It heated her up more than she'd ever been before. She couldn't wait to feel everything. Him surrounding her. Over her. Behind her as he moved within her.

He lowered her feet onto the bed while he stood at the base. This put them pretty much eye level. Now she could kiss him without him having to leap up and wrap herself around him.

She wanted to be around him; their bodies pressed so closely together it would be hard to tell where he ended and she started.

Their mouths came together. No need to talk. It was time to feel.

Tongues dueled, but in a teasing way that made their breathing rise to gasp around them.

She rubbed herself against him, and his fingers sought

her breasts, his claws grazing lightly across her nipples, making them pearl for him.

His tail, that wonderful tail, wound up her leg and stroked her slit. She dripped for him already, and his groan when his tail touched told her he knew and liked it.

His head lifted. "I need to taste you." Scooping her off her feet, he laid her down on the edge. Before her legs could drop to the floor, he'd ducked down between her thighs, pressing them wider with his hand and his tail.

"I am greedy," he snarled.

"Take whatever you want." She needed this moment with him, this time where nothing else mattered but them.

He growled and lowered his head. While one hand reached up to stroke her breast, his mouth claimed her.

His tongue glided up her slit and the tip of his tail rubbed her clit.

She bucked and keened. Damn, it was incredible. How could it get much better than this?

It could.

His thick tongue dove inside her, stroking her inner walls, licking at her juices while she squirmed and pressed her hips upward, seeking more.

Her head thrashed on the bed. Her hands gripped the blankets. And her legs splayed wider, letting him take whatever he pleased.

He licked and sucked while his tail rolled her clit, and she decided he could stay there, doing this for the rest of his life.

But tension climbed inside her, a rushing roar that would soon overtake her.

"I can't…" she cried, her hands tightened on the blankets. She bucked upward as his tongue plunged inside her, flicking and stroking and somehow finding her G-spot to tease.

It was too much. It wasn't enough.

She had to have it all.

"Likir. Please!"

He lifted his head and flashed his fangs her way. "Come for me. Show me how you can fall apart from my touch."

"I want you inside me."

"I will be, soon." With a flash of his fangs, his head dove downward.

His tongue thrust into her, his tail joining to flick against her inner walls while a thicker part of it continued to glide across her clit.

Her body tightened. The world lost focus.

The climax shook her, making her cry out.

He carefully licked her folds and inner walls while his tail teased her clit, driving her over the edge again and again until she was a limp wreck on the bed.

Looking up, he licked his lips and climbed over her.

His huge cock bobbed against his abdomen, and the dual thumb-sized nubs on the top and bottom vibrated softly, a subtle hum she couldn't wait to feel.

He lifted her legs by her heels, pulling her up as his body dropped down.

A swift thrust, and he embedded his thick, long cock inside her. It was almost too much.

Almost.

The stretch burned but in a good way.

And the nub on the top... Fuck, it felt amazing, latching onto her clit.

When he pulled out, the nub remained. She had to see this and with her hips lifted off the bed, him holding them up by his shoulders and spreading her wide, their connection was there for her to view.

There was something incredibly arousing about

watching his cock plunge forward, burying itself inside her, while the nub above somehow miraculously remained locked onto her clit, vibrating.

The other nub teased her butt, and she'd never done anything like that before. Soaked in her wetness, it inched forward, cresting the pursed lips with each thrust of his cock.

"Emily," he groaned, his body pumping. He lifted her up with each drive, and a heady feeling burst inside her, as if his soul reached out and touched hers.

Claimed hers.

He nudged her legs up as he bent forward, his body straining to move in a slow, careful manner. "You are so tight," he said hoarsely. "I don't want to hurt you."

"Don't hold back," she cried as he bent her, easing her heels near her head, an almost pretzel position that thrust her lower body up toward his. She spread herself wider, eager to take him all.

That nub on the bottom… It teased just inside, where nerve endings sparked to life for the very first time. A heady warmth filled her, and it surged through her body like an electrical jolt.

He moved within her, still too slow to give her everything she needed.

"Faster," she said, her hands clutching his arms. She moved her fingers across his chest and rubbed his nipples.

With a hoarse groan, he lost all control and pounded against her.

Yes, that was what she needed. Everything.

As she tugged on his nipples, his head thrust back. He growled before he buried his face in her neck. His fangs bit down, a pinch that shot her closer to the ecstasy she was seeking. She had to have it. Feel it.

His body surrounded her while he plunged in and

pulled out. The nubs above and below remained locked onto and inside her body, adding to her pleasure.

She spiraled closer, a coiled spring about to blaze into the sky.

His tongue smoothed across where he'd bitten, and he nibbled to her ear, where he bit down again.

She came in furious, rocking waves, her guttural cry mingling with his.

"Yes," he hissed. "Like that and more." He thrust harder, deeper, and she took everything he had to offer.

She was a greedy thing, determined to suck all of him deep inside her.

Her body crested and plunged upward again as another orgasm took her.

He groaned. His body shuddered.

And he shot everything he had inside her.

Likir

"Would you like another cinnamon bun?" Emily asked Likir the next morning.

"I ate five."

She grinned "They're small."

When he shook his head, she rose and took their plates to the sink. She turned and leaned against the counter.

"You cooked. I'll clean the dishes," he said.

Her snort came out of her, covered with her hand pressed against her lips. "I popped open the cylinder, placed them on the greased cookie sheet, and baked them. That's not exactly cooking."

He was still amazed. The slices she'd laid on the sheet of coo-kees appeared gooey and unappealing. But soon, an enticing aroma had filled the small dwelling, clawing at his senses. His belly had rumbled, and he felt weak, his energy sapped from claiming his mate all through the night.

Rising, he approached her, placing his palms on either side of her on the edge of the counter. He kissed along her jawline to her ear.

She shivered, and her sigh of pleasure echoed around them.

His cock rose, eager for another taste of her tight inner walls.

"Earth food preparation will never cease to amaze me," he said.

"I... What?" Her eyes popped open. "You're incredibly distracting."

"And you appreciate this in me."

"Hell, yeah, I do. But back to the conversation. Surely you cook food on Cu'zod sometimes. You don't replicate everything, right?"

Obviously, he was not distracting her enough. Last night, she'd slept in his arms and nightmares chased her. When he asked her softly to share her fears, she'd shaken her head. It gutted him that he couldn't soothe all her wounds and keep each tear from falling.

His tail entwined around her leg, seeking upward.

With a hitch of her breath, she opened her thighs, and he was grateful she wore a dress with nothing underneath.

"Everyone uses replicators on Cu'zod." He waved toward the counter. "It appears a bit like your microweave. We program what we want to eat, wait, and it is projected from the device, ready to be consumed."

Like he ached to consume her. He felt as if their time together would soon end. How could a matebond be forbidden?

Her face scrunching with uncertainty. "Does the food taste the same?"

"It tastes amazing." He captured her mouth, savoring the cinnamon still lingering on her tongue. "So do you."

"I thought you were going to do the dishes?" she said in a breathy voice. "I really should..."

"Should what?" he asked as he kissed along her collarbone and bit down on her shoulder.

"I, um..." She shook her head, and her tail of the pony swayed on her back.

He released the band, and her hair fanned around her shoulders. Burying his face in the silky strands, he groaned at the sweet scent.

"I think I want..." Her moan cut through the air as his tail teased her moist folds, seeking her clit.

In a flurry, her dress dropped to the floor, as did his pants. He'd come downstairs shirtless and with his feet bare to show her the weave between them.

She wrapped her hands around his cock, gliding her fingers along the surface. At the base, his blinder nubs vibrated softly, the motion transferring to his cock. A bead of precum coated the tip, and she bent down to lick it off, before taking him into her mouth.

Her hips spread, and his tail stroked up inside her. Her moan ripped through her, and she pressed back against his tail.

Their ragged breathing echoed around them.

Backing up, he shoved everything off the table, ignoring the clatter. All he could think of was her tight wetness surrounding him, taking everything he had to give.

He urged her to release his cock.

She pouted. "I wasn't done." Her pink tongue stroked her lips, claiming the precum as her own.

"And I'm not done with you yet, mate."

Her head tilted at the word, but she was soon distracted by him turning and bending her over the table.

Her ripe ass waited, her slit parted and gleaming.

One thrust, and he seated himself inside her. His blinder nubs got to work, one teasing between her ass cheeks, the other clinging to her clit as he moved.

Moaning and grasping at the table, she pushed back as he surged forward.

He couldn't get enough of her spread wide beneath him. Welcoming him.

The table banged against the wall as he plundered deeply, his cock thickening. Tightening.

Her orgasm burst from her, and she groaned against the surface of the table.

His cock surged, bunching, before he shot himself within her.

※

"I've never had cinnamon frosting on my boobs," Emily said with a laugh. She still lay beneath him and as far as he was concerned, they could remain in this position all day.

"I will gladly lick it off," he said.

"And I'll gladly let you."

When she wiggled, he backed away, his cock sliding out of her.

"Before you start licking, I need…" With a giggle, she ran toward the bathroom, snatching up her dress as she passed.

The doorbell rang, and she paused in the opening to the bathing quarters. Her shoulders curled forward. "I bet that's Bradley. Crap. Of course he won't keep his 'come by in the evening schedule'. I was hoping I'd never see him again."

That could be arranged.

"Would you like me to take care of this?" Likir could hand over the other tickets and maybe his fist while he was at it. His blood boiled whenever he thought of what this male had done to his precious mate.

"It's okay." She shot him a smile that held so much warmth, it made his chest hurt. "I can do this. You'll be with me during?"

"I will." He dragged on his pants and opted to continue shirtless and with nothing on his feet. Let Bradley gawk at his three toes instead of five. At his claws. At the proud scales marching across his exposed torso.

"Thanks. I won't be long." She ducked into the bathroom while he strode toward the front door.

"Oh, it's you," Brad-lee said, easing around Likir when he widened the panel. After the incident at the mall, this male was wise to be wary.

Brad-lee hurried into the living room, putting at least a tail's distance between them. Perhaps he wasn't so stupid after all. "Where's Emily? I didn't come here to talk to you."

"She will be here soon enough." Likir advanced on Brad-lee. "While we wait, we will get a few things settled between us." He held up his hand when Brad-lee started to speak. "First, you will never come here again. Second, you will leave Emily alone for the rest of her life. And third, you will apologize for causing her pain."

"You don't have any say in this," Brad-lee said, his face reddening and his hands clenching to fists at his sides.

"Oh, no?" Likir's tail rose and draped across the back of Bradley's shoulders, the tip gliding across the front of his throat.

"You can't threaten me. I have rights where you have nothing."

"Do not be so sure about that." While Likir had abdicated his role in the royal family, that did not mean he could be stepped upon, any more than any other Cu'zod. All Cu'zods had rights here on Earth, and Likir intended to assert them.

"What's going on?" Emily stood in the doorway between the kitchen and living room. "I assume you came for the tickets, Bradley?"

"Yes. Hand them over and I'll leave." His sneer took in Likir. "This asshole seems to think he can make demands."

"He *can* make demands," she said calmly, crossing over to put her arm around Likir. "He means everything to me."

"It's forbidden."

She shrugged. "We'll find a way around the rule. I plan to call the administrators this morning and begin an appeal process."

Smart thinking. Likir was proud of his mate.

"I won't permit it," Bradley blustered.

She laughed softly. "Like you have any say in this? You're the past, Bradley. I've moved on to someone better." Leaving Likir, she went to a small table standing along the wall with a metal bowl holding the original tickets. Likir had placed the new ones on his bureau, out of view Brad-lee's view. She turned and held them out. "Take them and leave. I don't want to see you or hear from you again."

"I withdraw my funding this instant!"

"Go ahead. I'll be sure to tell everyone about how you shoved a bunch of wounded animals out into the snow at Christmas. I'm sure your friends will be thrilled to hear that."

"They won't believe you."

She smiled, but it contained no humor. "Some will, and that's all that matters. You think you can hurt me, Bradley, but you can't. I won't let you."

"There are some things you can't control, Emily," he said.

Her chin lifted, and pride shone in her eyes. "I control

what I need to. If I didn't, I wouldn't have shoved you out of my life."

He stiffened. "I ended things between us."

Her laughter burst out. "You just keep thinking that if it makes you feel better."

With a growl, Brad-lee turned and stormed toward the door. But he paused with his hand on the knob. Turning with a slick grin spread on his face. "Has Likir told you his full name?"

She shrugged. "It's in all his paperwork."

"No, I meant his *real* name."

Blinking slowly, Emily turned to Likir, puzzlement rising on her face. "What's he talking about?"

Before Likir could explain himself, Bradley blurted it out.

"I'm not the only one who kept secrets from you, Emily. Allow me to introduce you to *Prince* Likir, second in line for the Cu'zod throne."

21

Emily

The world roared in Emily's ears, and she sputtered, unable to form words. Unable to think. She barely noticed Bradley leaving, slamming the door behind him.

"What's he talking about?" she asked in a croaky voice.

Why did everyone hurt her? Her fingers rose to her chest, where the pain pushed against her ribs.

"I was going to tell you eventually," Likir said, his voice soft and his hands splaying out at his sides.

"When?" They'd had sex together, multiple times. She'd shared everything with him, from the love she carried still for her grandmother, the hopes and dreams she had for her rescue, her absent parents, and every nasty thing Bradley had ever done to her.

While Likir... He'd withheld the core of who he truly was.

"I was going to tell you...soon."

A prince, huh? Of course. He was probably wealthy. Money changed things. Look at her parents, preferring to add to their bank balance than raise their daughter. And just like Bradley, Likir might take advantage of her, too.

In some ways, he already had.

She yanked on her coat and zipped it while Likir watched her. "I need to take a walk." A long walk, so she could think. "I..."

"Allow me to explain," he said, but how could he? He was a prince, wealthy, and he'd kept it from her. Nothing he could say would change that.

"I'll, um, it's okay." Not really, but she couldn't leave when it was clear from his cratered face that he was in pain, too. "I need a little time to think." Shaking her head, she stuffed her feet into her boots, grabbed Alfred's harness and leash, then carefully shut the door behind her. "I'll be back."

As she strode down her drive, her pup hopping along beside her, tears smarted in her eyes.

Everyone she trusted betrayed her.

Her feet stomped down the walk and took her around the corner. Ahead, the park waited with its tree-covered walkways and endless fresh air.

She needed to think, because...

Yeah, Likir kept something from her, but he didn't actually lie. He would never do anything to upset her. She was certain he had a reason for withholding the information, and when she got home after a breath or two of crisp air, she'd tell him she believed in him, that she knew he'd never hurt her.

And if he wanted to explain, she'd listen.

If he wanted to keep this part of himself private, she'd tell him she understood that, too. He didn't owe her anything he wasn't eager to give.

It hurt, yeah. How could it not? But a knee-jerk reaction would serve them no good. It would be so easy to slip into irritation that he'd kept this from her, to wallow in disappointment.

That was why Bradley told her. He wanted her to run, to shove Likir away.

Absolutely not.

They started their lives together when he had landed on Earth. Who he was before had been left behind.

He had a reason for keeping this from her, and she had a feeling it mattered.

She and Alfred walked slowly around the two-mile loop encircling the park, stopping for Alfred to do his business. He wanted to mark each tree and lantern post they came to, and she gave him the time he needed. Whenever he took a walk with her, he added another layer to his trust. He no longer flinched when her hand came near, and he gave kisses instead of growls. He'd healed.

Had Emily?

Perhaps not. Look at how she'd reacted to Bradley's well-planned reveal. He'd known she'd be upset to think Likir was keeping something from her, and he'd used it to cause her pain all over again.

What a complete bastard. She was so much better off without his toxicity in her life.

"Ah, so you're walking Alfred today?" someone said from behind her.

Emily turned and smiled at an older, white-bearded man she'd seen during walks in the past. He must live in her neighborhood. She bet he saw Likir walking Alfred. "Yes, it's this little doggie and me today."

"I'm Stanley, if I haven't mentioned that before."

She nodded. "Emily."

Alfred hopped around Stanley, yipping, and Emily gently tugged him back, closer to her leg.

"Is your friend still around?" Stanley asked.

"Likir? Yes, he is. He's back at my house."

"Oh, good." Stanley smiled. "Such a nice person. It's a joy to meet those coming here to start a new life. Immigrants help make the world a better place, don't you think?"

"I agree." And she couldn't wait to get home to him, to talk about how they were going to get rid of the rule keeping them apart. That was way more important than anything else.

"You seem stressed," Stanley said.

How could he tell?

"I'm a bit tense, but a walk is sorting everything out." Actually, everything would be sorted out when she got home.

"Good, good," he said, scratching his bushy beard. Other than being skinnier than a bedpost, he looked a lot like the Santa she'd pictured when she was little. But he must hear that a lot. It might irritate him if she brought it up. It wasn't like he was wearing a red and white suit and shouting ho, ho, ho at the top of his lungs. Just jeans, a down coat, and a light blue hat on his head. There wasn't a speck of Christmas about him other than his rosy cheeks and the sparkle in his merry eyes.

He started walking down the path, away from her. "I'll see you around another time, perhaps with Likir?"

"I'm sure you will," she said with a smile.

She needed to get back to Likir right away. They needed to talk.

"You do need to talk," Stanley called out.

She stared after him then shook her head.

Reading minds was for fairytales, not the reality she lived in.

"Come on, Alfred," she said, scooping up the pup to carry him. She could walk faster if she held him.

She hustled from the park, and it wasn't until she reached her house that she realized she didn't have to run. Her and Likir's conversation would happen when she got there, be it now or ten minutes later.

Silence greeted her when she stepped inside.

"Likir?" she called.

Frowning, she lowered Alfred to the floor and removed his harness. He hopped into the living room and jumped up onto the sofa, curling up on the fluffy blanket draped across the cushion. Valicia stretched and then rubbed against Alfred before settling against him for warmth.

Emily took the stairs to the second floor and nudged open the door to his bedroom.

No Likir.

Worse, his clothing was gone.

Her eyes prickled. She must be mistaken. He wouldn't have left her.

Racing downstairs, she ran out to the animal area. Cat meows and a few doggie whoofs greeted her, but no Likir.

She dragged herself back into the house, knowing what she'd find but not willing to face it. Her lungs hurt. She could barely breathe.

He'd left her?

After searching the house, she dropped down onto the couch beside Alfred and Valicia and tugged the kitten onto her lap. While the little beasty purred, Emily stared forward blankly.

He'd left her.

But... Color drew her eye to her elf costume sitting on the recliner seat opposite the coffee table.

Something had been placed upon it. Setting Valicia aside, she approached the costume, where she found one, solitary ticket to the Christmas Costume Ball.

In careful, rough handwriting, Likir had left her a note.

Meet me there?

22

Likir

While Likir did not believe in Earth tales of the fairy, every Cu'zod knew of legends that could not be explained. A creature who could fly without wings. A plant that could predict the future.

Warriors scoffed, stating the witnesses of these events must've had too much vebreen to drink.

Yet the tales persisted.

And now, Likir was confident he was riding in a vehicle with Santa.

"Are you sure they'll let you into the embassy?" His elderly friend, Stanley, also known as Santa in Likir's mind, said.

"I am."

After Emily took Alfred for a walk, Likir started thinking. He'd learned so much about Christmas during the time he'd been on Earth. And he'd learned there were nasty Earthlings like Brad-lee, just like on Cu'zod.

It was vital that Emily shine at the ball, and not for Likir or her or even to help him remain with her on Earth.

The animals were what mattered. She did such

amazing work. She deserved to keep making that difference in the life of other wounded creatures.

She told him she'd help him discover the true wonder of Christmas and he had. It came from doing something for others, those who were most vulnerable.

As for him and Emily, she made a solid point. There must be a way around the rule forbidding relationships between a Cu'zod and his or her sponsor.

This was something Likir thought he could fix. Emily would save the animals, and he'd save them.

The only person Likir knew who could fix this was his friend, the Cu'zod Ambassador to Earth, Trexon.

Yes, Likir could announce his former royal status, and he was confident the Earth government would listen to his plea to allow him and Emily to be together, but he'd cut ties with his royal status, and that meant no longer using his family name to make others do as he wished.

He came here to Earth to live like every other Cu'zod and none of them could announce former royal status and receive whatever they wanted.

That didn't mean Likir wasn't above speaking to friends who might be able to help. Trexon would not twist the rules for Likir, but he would speak with the Earth government on Likir's behalf, just as if he was a non-royal settler on this planet. Every Cu'zod could ask the Ambassador to advocate for them.

When he realized he needed to handle this before he and Emily could talk about a future together, he was determined to do it right away. He packed his things; knowing Bradley was going to force this with the administrator, Michael. If Likir didn't appear to live with Emily, it would be hard for anyone to accuse them of breaking the rules.

He also packed his elf costume and took his ticket, then left a note for Emily, asking her to meet up with him at the costume ball. Hopefully, by then, he'd have an answer about the rule.

Getting to the embassy was his only problem. Fortunately, almost as if by magic, he encountered Stanley on the walkway outside Emily's front door. When Likir asked how he could arrange transportation to the embassy, Stanley's bushy white eyebrows lifted.

"You'll need to take a flight to the capitol and then find transportation from there," Stanley said. "You'll be cutting it close if you want to get back by tomorrow for the Christmas Ball, though."

"Is it possible?"

Stanley's face creased with a smile. His cheeks were quite red from the cold, and Likir swore Stanley's eyes twinkled.

Truly, if this male wore a red and white suit, he could be Santa.

"Yes, it is possible," Stanley said. "Tell you what. I'll take you there myself."

And he had, arranging for tee-kets to ride in the aero-plane that terrified Likir the entire trip. How did Earthlings trust this simple device to keep them off the ground?

After their aero-plane landed, Stanley lifted his arm and a yellow vehicle magically appeared in front of them. Wonders never ceased. Stanley told the female driving the yellow car where they needed to go, and the female willingly took them to that location. More proof of Stanley—Santa's—magic.

Now, Likir stood outside the embassy, frowning at the Earthling guards who frowned back at him. He approached them, and their hands lifted to the weapons mounted on their sides. A stone wall encircled the embassy behind them, meshed with a steel fence that gleamed in the muted sunshine.

"I would like to speak with Trexon Roadas Valkaras," Likir said pleasantly.

The four guards looked at each other.

One laughed, his neck cricking back so he could look up at Likir. "Buddy, I can tell you're a Cu'zod, but any old Cu'zod can't stroll into the embassy to speak with the Ambassador. Do you have an appointment?"

Likir shook his head. "I do not, but I am confident he will speak with me." He peered over his shoulder at Stanley, who waved his hand Likir's way in encouragement. The yellow vehicle sat on the cab, its lights flashing rhythmically.

"If you don't have an appointment, I'm afraid you can't see him," another guard said kindly.

"I must."

"Call the embassy," the first said. "Set up an appointment, and come back then, okay?"

"Please allow me in. There is a vital matter I must discuss with Trexon."

Another guard rolled his eyes. "I'm sure there is." He extended a rectangular piece of paper to Likir. "Here's the main number to the embassy. Give 'em a call and they'll decide if your matter is important enough to arrange for an appointment with the Ambassador."

"It is." Likir pressed his fist against his chest. "I am not permitted to be with the female I…"

Ah, yes, he did.

His spine straightened, and his tail stiffened behind him. "I am not permitted to be with the female I love. I must speak to Trexon about the sponsorship rules."

The guard scowled. "We told you that's not possible. You need to leave before we call the authorities."

Likir growled, and the males universally lifted their weapons.

The last thing he wanted to do was cause an interstellar incident, but he had to speak to Trexon this day. As it was, he'd barely make it back in time for the ball.

Easing away, he returned to stand with Stanley.

While the older male must've overheard and knew Likir was forbidden entrance, Stanley smiled again. "Would you like me to talk with the guards on your behalf?"

What harm could there be in that?

"Thank you," Likir said, dipping forward in a bow. Frustration poured through him, but he couldn't think of anything he could do other than stride down the walk and find a place where he could scale the fence. But again, he didn't wish to cause trouble, just to speak with Trexon.

"Wait here," Stanley said. He strode casually over to the guards and spoke quietly. The guards peered around him, at Likir.

They frowned as one.

Stanley lifted his hand and touched the side of his nose, and then the 'it's-not-possible' miracle occurred.

One of the guards strode to the fence and opened it. He turned and stared at Likir with a dazed expression on his face. "Don't just stand there, buddy. Get inside."

Likir grinned at Stanley, whose eyes twinkled merrily.

"I'll wait here for you in the cab?" Stanley said, rubbing his arms. "It's chilly out and the heaters are blasting inside."

Likir strode over to Stanley and hugged him. "Thank you."

"Of course." Stanley patted Likir's arm. "One thing that may not make sense now, but don't worry about a certain mean Earthling male." He stepped back. "He's about to get a truckload of coal in his stocking."

23

Emily

To say Emily was a wreck was an understatement.

She stood outside the swanky country club entrance where the Christmas Costume Ball would be held, her ticket clutched in her hand. Alfred sat patiently on the cleared sidewalk beside her, looking incredibly cute in his doggie elf costume.

Why was she worried? Alfred would be the hit of the ball, and she could just sit back, hand out business cards, and bask in the pup's glory. Donors would beg to give her money to save the rescue.

A breeze skipped across the snow-covered green and scooted up under her felt elf skirt. Her skin peppered with goosebumps beneath her jingle bell tunic.

"Jingle bells, jingle bells," she sang in a low voice. "Jingle all the way."

"Excuse me, but do you plan to stand there all day or go inside?" Bradley said from her right.

She turned to see him and Bridget approaching, Bridget's leggy stride keeping pace with Bradley's. She wore a red wool coat and what looked like a Mrs. Claus costume beneath. Plus, a bonnet on her head that on Emily would make her look like she was eighty. Bridget rocked it like she starred in a Christmas movie.

As they approached, her gaze met Emily's, and Emily caught a hit of sadness there. And when Bradley reached for Bridget's hand, she evaded his touch.

Emily had a feeling that while Bridget might still be with Bradley, their relationship was on the way out.

More power to Bridget. Emily hoped she found someone new who'd be a step up from Bradley. Heaven knows, it wouldn't take much.

"I am going inside," Emily said when Bradley stopped beside her.

"Without a ticket?" he said with a sneer. "Are you planning to crash it?" He peered around her.

"No, I'm not crashing the ball."

Bradley held up the tickets he'd taken from Emily. "I threw the others away, and you're not getting in with these."

Emily stiffened. "I don't need your tickets."

"Bradley, enough," Bridget said, reinforcing Emily's belief that things were rocky between them. She didn't welcome pain on Bridget's part, but she did feel the woman deserved better.

"Where's your boyfriend?" His fingers clutched his red and white Santa suit. Really, he gave Santa a bad name.

"Likir will be here." Hopefully.

No, Emily would not lose hope. He indicated he'd come, and he would.

She trusted him—and that was such a welcome feeling. Finally, she'd found her own forever home with Likir.

"I bet he ditched you," Bradley said. "He's a prince. He can have whomever he wants, so why choose you?"

"Bradley!" Bridget cried, smacking his arm. "Jeez, talk about being mean."

"She isn't supposed to be with him," he said stiffly. "It's forbidden by the rules."

"Not true," someone said from behind Emily.

She turned to find her favorite elf standing behind her. Damn, he looked hot in his red and green suit they'd made together. His tail swished lazily behind him.

"Yes, a prince of Cu'zod can have any female he pleases, but I only want Emily." Likir's words might be for Bradley, but his gaze was solely for her.

"Likir," she said.

He strode closer, the bells on his hat, collar, and shoe coverings jingling merrily. Stopping in front of her, he held out his hand. "I believe we have a ball to attend, love, am I correct?"

"Love?" Bradley said with a snort.

"I love you, Emily, and if you feel the same, I want to spend the rest of my life with you," Likir said.

"Awww," Bridget said. "That's so sweet."

"This breaks the rules," Bradley snarled.

"Actually no," Likir said, his gaze never leaving hers. "It appears you didn't read the fine print."

Emily was no longer paying Bradley any attention. Who cared about a nasty ex when the real deal stood in front of her with his heart in his eyes?

"True mates are excluded from the rules," Likir said.

"True mates?" Emily's voice shook, overcome with emotion.

He held up his arm, showing the marking on his wrist. "Remember this? It means I am fated to be yours."

"That's so romantic," Bridget sighed. "I want a true mate."

"Earthling sponsors are allowed to develop relationships with Cu'zods if they are true mates," Likir said. "*We are not forbidden, and we never have been.*"

What she and Likir had together could never be denied by governments or Bradley.

"I love you, Likir," Emily said in a bold voice, unable to keep her grin off her face. "I only want to be with you."

"Then let us solidify your donors at the ball," he said.

She linked her hand through his arm. "I thought you'd never ask."

Alfred hopped around them, barking gaily, his little bells jangling. It was the happiest sound Emily had ever heard.

Tickets in hand, they strode around a sputtering Bradley and walked up to the country club entrance.

24

Likir

Outside the entrance to the large hall decked with lights and red and green bands of cloth, Emily and Likir handed a male their tee-kets.

Likir took Emily's hand. He turned her to face him and cupped her beautiful cheeks. "This is your chance to shine. Yes, I am a prince, and we will talk about why I kept that secret later. For now, this is about you advocating for the animals."

"I do love you, Likir. I meant it outside."

His heart essentially exploded, and he wouldn't have it any other way. "I love you, too." He couldn't wait to share everything with her. Then take her to bed.

"I believe some inside may speak of my former royal status," he said. "But this isn't about me. It isn't about us." His gaze fell on Alfred sitting beside them, his tiny tail spiraling. "It's about them."

"You'll be there with me?"

He could hear the shake in her voice. So much depended on what happened over the next hour or so, and he understood why she felt fear. "Always. Look for me and know I am there, supporting you in everything you say."

Her lower lip trembled, and her head jerked up and down.

While a female dressed in a candy cane suit watched them from the door with lifted eyebrows, Likir swept Emily off her feet and kissed her, putting everything inside himself in his kiss.

When he lifted his head, Emily gave him an easier smile.

"Keep doing that and I'm going to drag you into the coat closet and lock the door," she said.

He could not imagine what a coat closet was but being behind a locked door with Emily would be a dream come true. "Soon, mate," he said with complete pride.

"Mate? I like that." As she slid down his body, her smile took on a hint of mischief. "You sure you don't want to find that closet?"

His tail teased along her lower spine. "Go in there and let them see you create your own version of Christmas magic, my love."

She nodded, took a deep breath, and with Alfred's leash in hand, walked into the ballroom.

Likir followed and tucked himself along the wall to the right.

Lights had been strewn overhead and decorations dangled from the ceiling. An enormous green tree took up the far-right corner, decked in white lights and red and green balls. It wasn't as pretty as Grannie's tree. He was rapidly becoming partial to silver branches, not green.

There was no way a Cu'zod warrior could hide in a crowded room. If him towering over everyone else didn't draw attention, his tail, scales, and horns would.

No one approached him, however, though he wasn't sure why.

Maybe it was because Emily breathed life into the room. She looked amazing in her costume that was clearly crafted with love. Alfred skipped beside her, and everyone kept stooping down to give him pats. Each time they did, Emily would engage the person. Soon, her business card was in their hand, and they were smiling and nodding.

Success. He knew she could do it.

Emily shot him a grin, and it was clear her fear had fled. She'd found her confidence, and she didn't need him.

But she loved him. He'd heard her say it, and nothing could make him happier. He couldn't wait to take her home and show her everything she meant to him.

Then their real Christmas could begin.

About an hour into the ball, Emily found Likir. He stood near the bowl of pooch—no, punch—frowning at the pink contents. Blobs of something he couldn't identify floated across the top, spreading a milky white substance wherever they swam. Nothing could induce him to drink it.

"There you are," she said, excitement filling her voice. "This has been amazing."

He bent down to scratch behind Alfred's ears, and the doo-gee licked his hand.

"Things are going well?" he asked.

"I've not only made up the money Bradley withdrew, but I've doubled it," she cried. Her eyes shimmered. "Thank you."

"I did not do this, you did. The rescue is worthy, and you have the words to make it shine brighter than the lights above us."

She sighed, and her eyes gleamed. "Likir, you say the sweetest things."

He gave her a quick kiss. "Because you are the sweetest female I've ever known. You deserve the best."

"And that's you."

"You have me, then."

She grinned. "Yay."

"When you are finished, we will go home and celebrate our own Christmas," he said.

Emily leaped into his arms. "I can't wait."

"You say the word, and we will flee this pooch."

She frowned. "Pooch?"

He smacked his forehead. "Punch. Why is this pink liquid called something that means to hit?"

"That's a good question." Her giggle rang out. "I love how you make me laugh."

If he was lucky, he'd bring her joy for the rest of their days.

"I think we should go home and get that Christmas started, don't you?" she said.

A machine groaned overhead, and white flakes started falling down through the room, gathering on their shoulders.

"Snow," she said with a shake of her head. "Inside? I love it."

"And I love you."

As he spun her around, the flakes fell, and his mouth captured hers.

He had learned the meaning of Christmas. It was Emily. Him. Them.

Love.

25

Likir

"*Ho*, ho, ho," Likir said with a grin. He entered the kitchen, scooped Emily up in his arms, and spun her around.

She said this made her dizzy. But it also made her smile, so he wouldn't stop doing it.

He'd give his very heart to keep her smiling every day of her life.

"I've almost finished getting the veggie casserole ready. Just the last bit of cheese on top and I'll be done," she said when he lowered her to his feet.

"I have a present for you," he said.

"Aw." Her face fell. "I don't have anything for you. I meant to go shopping but we…"

Were in bed almost from the moment they returned from the ball.

"You gave me your heart and there is nothing I treasure more." He held up the small box crafted on Cu'zod. "I believe I mentioned I brought you something from my government. It is not a true gift from me, but more one from them."

"It's so pretty." Her head tilted as she stared down at the jeweled box in her hands. She looked cute in her red and green polka dot apron, though he really couldn't figure out why they were called polkas, which was an odd dance from Earth's past and had nothing to do with clothing worn for cooking.

"The mineral the box is made of is mined in the Blustair Mountains deep beneath the sea and combined with zedest wood cut on one of the islands." The pale lavender mineral was a beautiful contrast to the rich sparkly, brown wood.

"It's beautiful." She grinned up at him. "Thank you."

"Oh, the box is just a trivial thing."

"No it's not!" Her fingertip stroked the top. "It's amazing. I've never seen anything like it before."

"Open it."

With her mouth in a small O, she lifted the lid. Her eyes widened, and her finger hovered over them as if she was afraid to touch.

"What are these?" she asked in a breathy voice.

"They are also mined in the Blustair Mountains, deep beneath the sea."

"They look like precious jewels. The cuts... They sparkle but also seem to glow from the inside."

"Some say they contain a spark of ancient life," he said, pleased with her response to his family's gift.

They'd talked, and he'd explained why he hadn't told her his true identity. He was grateful she understood and supported him in keeping it quiet. They didn't know if Brad-lee would tell, but they decided to show no response if he did it. Brad-lee would not win.

"I can see why they say that." She gazed up at him with tears in her eyes. "They're gorgeous. Thank you."

"I thought we could…" He gulped; his voice cut off by nervousness. Him, a brave Cu'zod warrior, nervous?

He was.

"We could…?" she said, her eyes wide.

"You could select one, and we could have a pendant made with it."

She sucked in a breath and held it. "A pendant?"

"On Cu'zod, when a male asks his true mate to spend her life with him, he gifts her with a pendant made from a stone such as this."

"Likir," she said softly. Her eyes sparkled with unshed tears.

"Select one and make me the happiest Cu'zod on this planet?"

She lowered the box carefully onto the counter then took his hands and tugged him flush against her. "Yes, yes. But you should know that being with *you* makes me the happiest Earthling on this planet. I don't need anything else."

His mouth hovered over hers, and soon he'd kiss her until she was dizzy again. Then he would take her to their bedroom and show her all the love he held inside him for his tiny female.

But for now, all he could do was grin.

❄

I hope you enjoyed
Falling for an Alien Elf
as much as I enjoyed writing it.

Would you leave a review?
Your thoughts mean a lot to me!

If you haven't read
Snowed in with an Alien,
I've included Chapter 1 here…

About the Author

Ava Ross fell for men with unusual features when she first watched Star Wars, where alien creatures have gone mainstream. She lives in New England with her husband (who is sadly not an alien, though he is still cute in his own way), her kids, and a few assorted pets.

Books by AVA

MAIL-ORDER BRIDES OF CRAKAIR

Vork

Bryk

Jorg

Kral

Wulf

Lyel

Axil, Gaje

(Companion novellas)

❄

BRIDES OF DRIEGON

Malac

Drace

Rashe

Teran

Kruze, Allor, Skoar

(Companion novellas)

ALIEN EMBRACE ANTHOLOGY

Skoar

(A Brides of Driegon novella

available for a limited time)

FATED MATES OF THE FERLAERN WARRIORS

Enticed by an Alien Warlord

Tamed by an Alien Warlord

Seduced by an Alien Warlord

Tempted by an Alien Warlord

Craved by an Alien Warlord

XILAN WARRIOR'S MATES

Alien Commander's Mate

Alien Prince's Bride

Alien Hunter's Prize

Alien Pirate's Plunder

On Kindle Vella

HOLIDAY WITH A CUZ'OD WARRIOR

Snowed in with an Alien

Falling for an Alien Elf

You can find my books on Amazon.

Snowed In With An Alien

With Christmas approaching, can Aida and Trexon give an orphaned little girl her holiday wish, plus find the perfect ending for themselves?

Before her conniving father can steal her orphaned niece away, Aida's determined to give the three-year-old child the Christmas she's been wishing for. Aida grabs the girl and runs, but her daring escape to a mountain cabin during a freak blizzard lands her in trouble. She's stuck in a cabin, there's no hope of a jolly Christmas in sight, and she stumbles over a wounded Cu'zod alien warrior. The storm keeps them snowbound, and between making snowmen and trimming the tree with Trexon, she starts dreaming of a future for both her and her niece.

En route to a diplomatic mission, Trexon crash lands on Earth in the middle of a snowstorm. He soon finds himself stumbling through the cold. A beautiful Earthling female rescues him, and she takes him to her isolated cabin, where he falls for her sweet ways. After he learns of their plight, he's determined to make Aida and the child's holiday wishes come true. But once the storm is over, Trexon must sign the treaty and take a one-way flight back to Cu'zod. If he goes, he'll lose his fated mate, but if he stays, the Earth-Cu'zod alliance could be lost forever.

Snowed in with an Alien is the first in a series of alien holiday romances that will release periodically. This standalone, full-length romance has on-the-page heat, aliens who look and act alien, a guaranteed happily ever after, lots of humor, no cheating, and no cliffhanger.

Chapter 1
AIDA

"How dare you bring that... that alien thing into my home?" Aida's father shouted from where he sat on his sofa in the living room of his palatial home.

"Mean man," Pansy whispered, pressing her back against Aida's legs. The child's tail coiled around Aida's leg, holding on.

While Aida didn't disagree with her three-year-old niece, she didn't have the nerve to speak as frankly with her father. Actually, she'd never had the nerve.

Until he turned his rage on Pansy.

"Pansy's not a thing," Aida said, her voice tight with indignation. Standing in the doorway to his living room, she braced Pansy's shoulders, hoping the child would think he meant someone else, and not her. "She's Tory and Zikane's child. An amazing little girl. Tory and Zikane loved her."

"Zikane," he huffed. "What kind of name is that?"

"A Cu'zod name. You know that."

Like every other time Aida spoke with her dad, her hands shook, and she struggled to keep from reaching a boiling point. He'd been able to reduce her to a crumbling heap from the time she was two. It looked like today wouldn't be any different.

"Cu'zod," he snarled.

His gaze took in his wife, Sandy—Aida's stepmom—sitting on the sofa beside him. She couldn't take her eyes off Pansy, though Aida couldn't read her facial expression.

"I've said it over and over again," he said. "We don't need relations with these cursed aliens."

The Cu'zod weren't cursed. They were people, just like those living on Earth.

Four-and-a-half years ago, an alien spaceship landed on Earth and three males emerged, Zikane and his two friends. Earthlings reacted to the alien's arrival in a variety of ways.

Aida's sister, Tory, worked near the landing site. When the ship streaked across the sky, she ran to see what was going on. She greeted them and soon fell in love with Zikane.

The other two males were captured. They came in peace and were greeted with kidnapping. If the government hadn't intervened and freed them, allowing them to return to Cu'zod, who knows what would've happened.

Zikane was given permission to stay with Tory, but the government put their foot down. No one was allowed to travel to Cu'zod, and no more Cu'zods were permitted to come to Earth.

Zikane and Tory married and had Pansy. Six months ago, it all fell apart.

"Pansy's your granddaughter," Aida said, her spine tight. "She needs us now, more than ever." Her heart ached all over again for their loss. Her sister! Gone forever. Sometimes, it just didn't seem possible.

"What kind of name is Pansy, anyway?" Charles

Weston the third said, rising from the sofa. He carefully placed his snifter of brandy on the low table beside the couch and smoothed back his dark hair only now beginning to thread through with silver. With a disgusted grunt, he strode toward where Aida still stood with Pansy, in the doorway of the room.

She hadn't dared to enter his sanctum. Why *had* she come here?

Oh, yes, the holidays. Christmas was only a few days away. Last night, Aida rocked Pansy to sleep while the child cried for her parents. Aida promised her a special Christmas. She'd thought it would be even more special to include her dad and stepmom. So much for that idea.

Despite their lifelong conflict, Aida had hoped her father could find a scrap of love in his heart for his orphaned grandchild, even if he couldn't find it for his youngest daughter.

Sandy glanced back and forth between them, and Aida swore her stepmother's eyes softened when they landed on Pansy. "Now, now, Charles. Let's not be hasty."

Aida's stepmom might love Dad, but it was clear love didn't blind her to his faults. His stubbornness was one.

His hate for Aida, another. He'd despised her since Aida's mother died after Aida fell into the swimming pool and Mom rescued her. He'd blamed her for the accident ever since.

It appeared he would pile his loathing onto Pansy as well, solely because of who her father was.

Relations with the alien Cu'zod species were still in great turmoil, and attitudes like his weren't making things better. Some Earthlings wanted the Cu'zods on Earth so they could conduct research on them. Others hoped to profit off the technology the Cu'zods generously offered.

Thankfully, a rising number among the rest of the population wanted peace between the two worlds.

That's why they were about to sign a new treaty.

"Sandy, you don't understand," Dad said, his tone lightening. When he turned back to Aida, his gaze sharpened again. "This...thing should not be in our home. I would like you to leave."

His attention fell to Pansy, and he reached out to poke the tiny, pale blue horns jutting up from her forehead. That and her lightly scaled blue skin were the only characteristics she inherited from her father.

Her petite frame, dimpled chin, and pert nose came from Tory, and it wrenched Aida's heart sideways whenever she saw them. She missed her sister so much.

"This..." he snarled. "I cannot allow this to remain in my home."

"Wanna leave," Pansy said, turning to hide her face in Aida's pants. "Want Ixmas."

"She's not a *this*," Aida protested, stroking Pansy's lush black hair so like Aida's own. But she could see her words were making no headway with her father. "She's a sweet child. She misses her mom and dad. I wanted..." She hated that her voice broke. Somehow, she'd thought Pansy might make a difference with him. So foolish of her. "I guess it doesn't matter what I wanted."

Aida was determined this child would not grow up the way Aida had. Other than Tory's kindness, Aida's childhood had been a stark, lonely existence. She left home when she turned eighteen. Things hadn't been easy for her after that, but she'd gotten an education and her life was looking better every day.

There was room in her life for Pansy.

As for her father? She'd tried. It didn't appear he would meet her halfway.

"Just one moment," Sandy said, rising from the sofa. She crossed the room to join them and linked her hand through Charles's arm. She leaned into him with true affection. "This could be the only grandchild we'll ever have."

Interesting way to put it.

It was hard for Aida not to bristle. At twenty-eight, she still ached to have a family who loved and cared for her. Sandy had always been polite, though distant, but she hadn't been a bridge between Aida and her father.

As for giving them grandkids? Aida hadn't met the right guy but hoped someday to welcome someone into her heart.

"Her name's Pansy, you say?" Sandy asked, and despite her kind tone, a shiver tracked down Aida's spine, though she couldn't name why. Sandy bent forward and held out her hand to the child. "Would you like to sit with me on the sofa?"

Pansy's fingers tightened on Aida's pants.

"Such a sweet name," Sandy said.

"Tory loved flowers," Aida said in a reasonable tone. "As you know, she owned her own landscaping business."

When Tory and Zikane died in the fire that ripped through the business six months ago, Pansy was at daycare. Someone contacted Aida, and she stepped in and claimed her orphaned niece. She had guardianship for the moment, and the paperwork solidifying the adoption of her niece was still being processed.

"I see," Sandy said, straightening. "Charles..." She couldn't take her attention off Pansy.

Aida's mouth went dry at the covetous expression filling Sandy's icy blue eyes.

"We should go," Aida said, taking her niece's hand and inching backward into the front hall. "Pansy and I are going to have a wonderful Christmas, but we need to leave for the cabin I've rented soon."

She gave up the idea of inviting them. If he was so determined to reject Pansy, he could spend his holiday with Sandy.

"Perhaps..." Sandy tapped her chin, her pretty features tightening. She paced after them, into the foyer. "I'm unable to have children, as you know."

Aida didn't know this, but why would she? She'd gone to their wedding but was seated at the reception with a few distant business associates, as if she wasn't truly family. She'd only met her new stepmother once for a short walk in the park, and another time at a coffee shop where Sandy politely told Aida she was welcome to visit but to not overstay her welcome.

She pointedly said that Aida's father didn't like having her around.

Sandy's ability to have children hadn't come up in the short conversation. Why bring it up now?

Oh.

Aida's fingers tightened on Pansy's, as if that would keep Sandy from snatching the child away.

"She has no other relatives?" Sandy said, her penciled brows lifting.

Dad frowned and tilted his head his wife's way. "Please tell me you are not thinking of anything like that."

Fear bolting through her, Aida tugged Pansy toward the front door. She was stupid to come here, because now she'd revealed this wonderful child to her father and stepmother.

"Not so fast," Dad called from the doorway to the living room. His gaze remained focused on Pansy. Instead of disgust, Aida read a covetous expression in his eyes. "Tory always was my favorite child."

He'd made that abundantly clear.

Sandy glided her arm around the back of his waist. Her face tightened, conniving. Why had Aida ever believed this woman could create something special between Aida and her dad?

"I think we should petition the court, don't you, Charles?" Sandy said. "Surely we'll be able to provide the best life for this poor child. We're wealthy and Aida...is not."

Money didn't mean much if a heart didn't come with it. And Aida did okay. She had an accounting job that paid well, and she was saving to buy her own condo.

"I'm raising Pansy," Aida said stiffly. "I'm her guardian. I've applied to adopt her, and the judge said—"

"Judge Trudell?" Charles bit out.

"Yes," Aida said, her fingers trembling on the front doorknob.

"You still have the judge's number, don't you?" Sandy asked. She stepped forward, holding out her hand. "Petunia, dear, why don't you come with me? We have six lovely bedrooms upstairs, and you can choose the one you love most for your own."

"Her name is *Pansy*," Aida said.

"No..." Pansy slunk behind Aida, clinging to the back of her pants. "Wanna stay wit Auntie Aida."

"Release the child," Dad said. "You do not have the means to raise her yourself."

Aida shook her head, her dark hair spilling across the front of her red and green Christmas sweater. It was a silly thing, and she'd thought her father might laugh at the cute phrase scrolled across the front. No, she'd hoped they'd laugh together.

So much for that wild idea.

"You can't have her," Aida said, her chin lifting.

As her dad stormed toward her, his hands outstretched like claws, she turned and wrenched the front door open.

She and Pansy fled into the snowy night.

>
> You can get your copy of
> Snowed in with an Alien
> on Amazon.

Made in United States
Orlando, FL
03 December 2023